THE LEGACY SERIES

SERIES TITLES

Adult Children
Laurence Klavan

Guardians & Saints
Diane Josefowicz

Western Terminus: Stories and A Novella
Michael Keefe

Like Human
Janet Goldberg

The Hopefuls
Elizabeth Oness

Never Stop Exiting
Michael Hopkins

Broken Heart Syndrome
Anne Colwell

The Mexican Messiah: A Novella & Stories
Jay Kauffmann

Close to a Flame
Colleen Alles

American Animism
Jamey Gallagher

Keeping What's Best Left Kept Secret
David Ricchiute

Soaked
Toby LeBlanc

The Machine We Trust
Tim Conrad

Gridlock
Brett Biebel

Salt Folk
Ryan Habermeyer

The Commission of Inquiry
Patrick Nevins

Maximum Speed
Kevin Clouther

Reach Her in This Light
Jane Curtis

The Spirit in My Shoes
John Michael Cummings

The Effects of Urban Renewal on Mid-Century America and Other Crime Stories
Jeff Esterholm

What Makes You Think You're Supposed to Feel Better
Jody Hobbs Hesler

Fugitive Daydreams
Leah McCormack

Hoist House: A Novella & Stories
Jenny Robertson

Finding the Bones: Stories & A Novella
Nikki Kallio

"Disturbing, surprising, and unflinchingly intimate, Laurence Klavan's stories make the mundane bizarre and are absolutely engrossing."

—DANICA NOVGORODOFF
author of *The Undertaking of Lily Chen*

"Wonderfully strange tales—cunningly written—eerie and satiric by turn—often evoking tremendous pathos."

—DAVID GREENSPAN
Obie Award winner
author of *The Myopia*

ADULT CHILDREN

stories

LAURENCE KLAVAN

CORNERSTONE PRESS

UNIVERSITY OF WISCONSIN-STEVENS POINT

Cornerstone Press, Stevens Point, Wisconsin 54481
Copyright © 2025 Laurence Klavan
www.uwsp.edu/cornerstone

Printed in the United States of America by
Point Print and Design Studio, Stevens Point, Wisconsin

Library of Congress Control Number: 2025943470
ISBN: 978-1-968148-10-2

Cornerstone Press titles are produced in courses and internships offered by the
Department of English at the University of Wisconsin–Stevens Point.

DIRECTOR & PUBLISHER
Dr. Ross K. Tangedal

EXECUTIVE EDITORS
Jeff Snowbarger, Freesia McKee

EDITORIAL DIRECTOR
Brett Hill

SENIOR EDITORS
Paige Biever, Eva Nielsen, Reilly Crous

PRESS STAFF
Jacob Childress, Karlie Harpold, Kimberly Janesh, Mai Yer Lee, Abby Paulsen,
Sam Zajkowski, Mydasia Zipperer, Samantha Bjork, Sophie McPherson, Madison
Schultz, Autumn Vine

For Susan

Stories

Obsolescence

It hadn't been intentional, Cody thought. Had it? He wasn't self-analytical, a trait he'd inherited from his father, the man he'd "forgotten" to invite to his bachelor party.

Why was that part of the tradition anyway? Cody wondered. You asked your best pals and brothers (if you had any; he didn't; he was an only child), but your father? It would have been strange and constricting to have the old man there. Wouldn't it?

Not that there had been anything salacious about the event. On the contrary, it had reflected not just Cody's beliefs but those of his fiancée Lona. No strippers or hookers or whomever one used to employ to bid farewell to being single, to the sleaziest sense of being single. In fact, the party had been designed for Cody *by* Lona, who had used her gifts as a reporter on sustainability to make it a statement on the subject, a display of the dos and don'ts of leaving as fleeting a footprint as possible on the world.

The refreshments were single portions of crispy organic fruit snacks (coconut chips, pineapple and mango slices) packaged in bags made from paper cellulose laminate and adorned with funny fruit characters. The wine was made from natural wastewater filled with plants scrubbing it clean with their roots. Even the location (a tiny free-standing 186-square foot structure) was "cargotecture," built from recycled shipping containers designed to be dismantled and reconfigured after just one use.

Cody thought his father might not have approved. After all, Tremaine was an old school person, a retired city planner, widowed, privileged, and inexpressive (though he possessed a quiet and impish sense of humor he revealed just in an occasionally muttered aside which seemed to even take him by surprise).

Cody apologized to his father for the lapse, unsure if he'd have been better off saying nothing and not opening the wound.

"It's fine," Tremaine said, shrugging and not meeting Cody's eyes, as he almost never did.

"You sure?" Cody said.

"About not being invited? Absolutely. Don't be silly."

"Good. I'm glad." And he really was relieved.

Cody made sure to give him a goody bag from the party and to invite him to the wedding right then and there.

That event was held outdoors at a national park, to avoid unnecessary use of private resources. Lona ordered even more edifying accoutrements: plates and cutlery made of biodegradable corn, menus from seed paper that could be planted as flowers, non-toxic candles, latex balloons, and bubbles instead of confetti. There was an eco-conscious registry in which stainless steel straws, silicone cupcake liners, and metal tea bags were requested. Cody's and Lona's rings were made from Moissanite, a rare, naturally occurring mineral that was conflict-free.

For a while, Cody worried that his dad might not show up. The initial meet-and-greet was over and the ceremony was about to start when Tremaine finally appeared.

From feet away, Cody waved to him over another guest's back. The old man nodded in return, looking suave in a trim black overcoat he was beginning to remove (truthfully, it was too cold for an outdoor event). Cody returned his attention to the person he was addressing. Then he did what in the dead days of show business would have been dubbed a double-take.

The invite had called for "casual dress." His father—always physically modest—wore no jacket or tie, just a white dress shirt and jeans. More than one button on the shirt was undone, and Cody saw something around and above his Adam's apple.

It was the digital "scarf" included in the bachelor party goody bag (the device had been included, anyway, which activated the virtual accessory). Circling a person's neck like the headlines in the old Times Square tickertape, the "scarf" was timed to change color, size and texture as it revolved. By not using and wasting cloth it was not bound to decay, require a replacement, and clog the environment. Unlike an actual scarf, it would never become obsolete.

His father's wearing it was weird enough, like an old guy sporting a Nehru jacket and love beads in the sixties or—what?—a fur coat while strumming a ukulele in the twenties. It was the *way* he wore it, the way he wouldn't let you forget that he did.

Tremaine usually strode in a march-like manner: knees up, back straight, arms at his side. Now through the wedding party, he sidled in the most attention-getting, focus-pulling style, his thumbs poking obnoxiously at himself and his "attired" neck.

"Hey!" Cody heard his father call from as far away as he stood. "Hey, everybody! Look at me!"

Suddenly, Cody was reminded of the snakes-in-a-can that kids opened up, containers that seemed too impossibly small to hold all the anarchy inside. His father's lid had been lopped off and look what was springing out.

"Hey! Hey…" Now his dad was using young person's slang that Cody hadn't even known he knew. They were expressions that—no matter what they meant—coming from him sounded acerbic, sarcastic, and snide.

"Excuse me," Cody said, mortified, to whomever he was no longer concentrating on, "I have to go and…"

But it was too late. The part-priest, part-rabbi (prabbi) who was officiating at the service had placed her hand on his shoulder, telling him it was time.

All through the ceremony, Cody and everyone else were distracted by the unmistakable sight and sound of his father, still resentfully parading, pointing at himself and parroting young people's talk, not stopping as the scarf around his neck did not stop.

This turned out to be an omen for his marriage. Within months, Cody and Lona found themselves at odds, largely (Lona believed) due to Cody's inability to grow, adapt, and change. He still hung out with his male friends, carried on with women as if free, caroused, and came home late.

"You don't live alone anymore, you know," Lona said, after (she believed) Cody had been selfish, distant, or actually absent too many times.

"I know that," he said, defensively.

"Do you? Do you know that you're married now?"

"Of course. What kind of a question…"

"You know that you're not a child anymore, but a man? Are you sure?"

Though he promised to improve, Cody (at least in Lona's eyes) did not. For his part, he began to believe his new wife was an overbearing presence, maternal in the worst way, someone who made him do what he did not want to do all day long.

Late one night, Cody landed at his father's house. He was intending—at least this was how he had left it with Lona—to "cool off for a while."

"But what *happened?*" Tremaine asked, squinting while he made up his guest room (as he did so often now, he'd dozed off reading). He was back to his old patrician manner and his uniform of a black James Bond-style turtleneck and Chinos.

"It's a long story," Cody said, not wanting to complain, blame Lona, or recall how she'd blamed him. "I think I'd just like to sleep now, if you don't mind."

"I don't mind. Mi casa…" Tremaine left the rest of the expression hanging. Either the old man assumed Cody knew it or he'd forgotten, Cody wasn't sure.

Soon Cody was unconscious, soothed by being in a big bed in a room beside his father's.

He woke up, suddenly, weeping in the middle of the night. He couldn't remember the bad dream that had jolted him, but he could feel tears like escaped prisoners falling off his chin, sliding down his clavicle and hiding in the hair on his chest. His heart beat so hard it hurt.

"Dad?"

Cody wandered into the room next door, groping in the darkness like a ghost before his eyes adjusted. He found his father's bed, bumping the old man's feet as he sat down. Had he just spoken, addressed Tremaine, in a whisper? He didn't know. In any case, the old man hadn't awakened.

Cody felt close to him now—and not just physically. Was this why he'd "forgotten" to invite him, because he couldn't face how similar they were, a fact he now longed to embrace? Or had Cody simply not known it yet? The two were determined to remain as they were, to be as permanent as food preserved in plastic packages. His wife and her ilk had tried to remove and replace them, but they would not succeed, not while Cody had something to say about it, which would be forever.

"Dad?"

Now Cody *had* spoken, in a voice as small and breaking as a boy's. He snapped the switch on the cord of his father's bedside lamp, the Art Nouveau light he'd always owned—only its bulb, like a beating heart, had ever been replaced.

Cody's father lay on his back, wearing an open plaid pajama shirt. The digital scarf still spun around his neck and had circled ever tighter until it strangled him. By staying the same, he had become permanently obsolete. His eyes bugged as if he'd realized he'd made this most basic and primal error. Tremaine's lips parted and puckered as if blowing a kiss or starting to say Cody's name or calling goodbye to his beloved son.

Endless

They called it The Endless Need, but the baristas cut you off at some point like selfish parents who wanted more for themselves. Regal had learned this when he'd requested a fourth refill and been rebuffed. Still, he kept coming there—because it was the only coffee place on his burned-out block? Hard to say.

Today he saw the woman again, the other regular, who wore a cap inside no matter what the weather. It shaped her face like the close-up of a silent film star (he'd subscribed to a channel that showed that stuff when he'd had the money). Had he kept coming to see *her*?

Regal felt thick liquid start to drip from his hair again, like what those silent film stars called pomade. He pressed a tiny napkin square to absorb it, of course to no avail. It was resistant to any cleansing agent. Then he stuck out his tongue to get the last drop of coffee from his finite cup.

Had Regal come straining for sustenance, because his mother had just died and food and feeding reminded him of her?

Food had always been an issue with his mother, who'd been called Brenda, a name he'd never used. An "issue"— right, Regal thought: her hunger was non-existent. She seemed never to place a piece of food in her mouth yet survived, looked svelte, even stylish—healthy, if nothing else. His father had spent his life saving her, serving her… something. In secret? What? Regal had never known until recently, when his father died and left him alone at thirty-five and living with her.

Once his father Bernard was gone, his mother's appearance and condition had changed. Quickly, she'd gone from hearty to halting, from a brisk step and booming voice to a weak gait and rasping whisper. She became, in fact, like someone starving to death.

With the same useless and now disintegrating square, Regal dabbed at what he'd imagined was sweat on his upper lip. It was really more of the viscous discharge which defied being dried.

"Don't you want to eat something?" he'd asked his mother one day, trying to speak above the sound of her wheezes.

"No," she could barely reply.

"How about a glass of juice?"

Brenda had shaken her head, which seemed to take forever and further exhaust her. Then she fell deeper into the bed on which they were sitting and lay flat, one foot waving shakily above the floor like a clapper in a broken bell, while she stared at the ceiling.

"If only…" she started to say.

"What?" He could hardly hear her.

"If only your father was alive."

"Well, he's not."

Regal wasn't emotionally intuitive, yet he sensed this answer was unsatisfactory. It made him as enervated as Brenda. He did not know how to help her and assumed it was hopeless to even try.

Then his mother's bathrobe (which she'd been wearing nonstop since Bernard's death) shifted and opened. Had she undone the sash so it would? Regal thought she might have, which was weird. His mother wore nothing underneath.

Apparently, she wanted him to see her, for she jerked one leg to further separate the sides of the robe.

"Mom," Regal said, discreetly, hoping she knew it meant to cover up.

Yet Brenda didn't stir. If it was possible, she lay even flatter, as if to invite inspection. Soon Regal was too curious and confused not to glance over and check her out. Then he could not keep from staring.

A chasm was visible in his mother, from her sternum to her gut. It was as dark as something too dark to be described. As dark as death? That was always said to be dark, wasn't it? Darker than *that*, Regal thought. There was no end to it, as there was no surcease to outer space, scientists suggested. Neither of these comparisons cut it, Regal thought—it was unique, itself alone. Regal looked up slowly, trepidatiously, at his mother's face.

"If only your father was alive," she repeated.

This time, she eyeballed him, as if to say: Got it? Then she darted a look at the vast, unquantifiable canyon that was in herself.

As if someone had whispered the answer in his ear, Regal understood. Whomever had whispered seemed to push him once, twice, three times until he did what his mother wanted—which was to fall, dip, do whatever it was called when a scuba diver tipped from a small boat and sank into an ocean.

Unlike an ocean, though—the interior and inhabitants of which were wet, visible at least with goggles, and gently rocking or wildly whooshing, depending on the waves—the atmosphere inside was at most moist, utterly black and totally silent. Soon something was conspicuously, consistently, and painlessly sucking at him as, yes, as a school of fish—one concession to the other comparison—nibbled for nutrition.

His mother was feeding on him as she had fed upon his father all those years.

Regal woke up alone in the bed. For a second, he believed he had imagined the whole thing, had a dream that, while not nasty, was not so nice. When he became completely conscious, he heard the shower running behind the bathroom's closed door. With a squeak of rusty knobs, it was switched off. Then his mother emerged, hair wet, robe closed, with a pep in her step.

"Everything okay?" she asked.

Without waiting for an answer, she strode out. Regal had responded with just a wan thumbs up before his hand fell to his side.

This was when he first felt thick liquid slide from his brow down the ramp of his nose and into his mouth. It had the texture and (he imagined) taste of hand sanitizer. He realized that, in small deposits, the stuff was all over him, the residue of the place inside his parent where he had served as supper.

This was what Regal tried to wipe away at The Endless Need. He looked at the woman in the cap and—shocking him, for the first time, for an instant—she looked back.

Several times a day, Regal had continued to serve as sustenance for his mother. For a while, it made a difference: his elder was invigorated, returned to a semblance of the shape she'd been in before her spouse's death.

It didn't last. Soon it became clear to Regal that the daily sessions (which left him weak but otherwise unharmed), his being Brenda's three squares, was not succeeding, not sticking to her ribs. She began to slip back into the skeletal form she had assumed weeks earlier, no matter how often Regal allowed himself to be absorbed by her.

"If only your father was alive," she said once more, the second before she died.

After he buried her, Regal assumed that the substance that stained him would disappear. Yet it did not: it still stuck to and seeped out of him, no matter what he did.

Now he crumpled up what was left of the damp and useless napkin. Before leaving the coffee shop, he gave a final glance across its shabby interior at the woman upon whom he'd been spying. Then he knew why she always wore the cap.

Her own goo was oozing from beneath it.

She was better prepared, Regal thought, dabbing upon it a dainty handkerchief retained for this purpose. She had no more success than he, yet the expensive cloth didn't collapse.

Regal couldn't stop himself. He rose from his stool and moved across the discolored tiles to her side. The woman looked up, startled, at what she feared was an attacker. Instead, she saw a presentable—if pale, pudgy, and balding—man her own age stop and point imperatively at his dripping face. Then she smiled.

Her name was Maribeth and her father had just died.

"And..." Regal was excited and interrupted her, "you always wondered how he stayed alive, because..."

"He never ate."

The two were in the street. They had been asked to leave by the barista, for Regal had been too loud, even though the place was otherwise empty.

"And in your father, you found..." This was Regal again.

"A giant hole."

"Yes."

"Unending."

"And *you* fed it, until you discovered..."

"That I wasn't enough."

"Only the other parent..."

"Could satisfy the hunger."

"And now..."

"I can't get it off me."

Maribeth indulged Regal's overwrought approach, being less high-strung than he was and equally glad to have met. After both stopped nodding, they simply stood on the strip, amid hordes of homeless people and the mentally ill. When the number grew too great, Maribeth suggested they head for her apartment, which was nearby.

There one thing led to another.

"I assume," Maribeth said, starting a third glass of wine, "people like us have always been around…"

"We just…" Regal's interruptions had become less frequent and ferocious, slowed by the alcohol.

"…never noticed."

"Uh huh."

With Regal not used to drinking and nearly sedated, Maribeth had to make the first move. She came close and her shift caused a splash of parental insides to jump from her hair to his (she had nearly shaved her head to free her scalp and fit better beneath a cap).

Then they stopped, nose to nose.

"Why…" Maribeth began, as Regal nodded at her to continue, "didn't our parents look like this?"

She meant sticky, for they hadn't. Regal shrugged: it was exactly what he was wondering.

When they started kissing—Maribeth went first and Regal followed— they had their answer. The stuff came off the other into their mouths, and it tasted good, or they had grown too excited to care how it tasted. Just as their parents had apparently done for decades, they licked and sucked and loved each other clean.

A month later, they were married. In the small civil ceremony, they promised love until death, which was as close to endless as there was on Earth. Afterwards, they realized their lives together would be better than their parents'.

"I'm hungry," they said, and for actual food. They had spoken at the exact same time and blurted out…

"Bread," Regal said.

"And butter," Maribeth said.

Spirit

"What do you mean, he doesn't know who you are?"

"I have to introduce myself."

"How often?"

"Every day."

"Jeez."

Hal hadn't known it had gotten this bad. His father's live-in nurse—whom the old man had employed for a year—was a familiar face.

"Sorry about this."

"It's my job," Jalene shrugged.

Hal was surprised she didn't have more of an investment in caring for his father. Still, maybe Jalene had steeled herself against the very thing starting to happen—the way you broke up with people before they broke up with you, hardened your heart, as it were.

"I'll come by tomorrow," he said.

"Okay. What time, though? I have to get my kid to the shrink."

"From two to four? You can take off, don't worry."

"Thanks!"

Jalene's tone said she thought Hal was a great guy, which he appreciated. He knew it wasn't true: he had become less likable as time had gone on, seen his wife leave (after he was unfaithful), lost the love of his kids, twelve and fourteen (whom he'd ignored). A little praise—even if unfelt, even if he had pandered to receive it—went a long way.

Jalene was devoted to a violent teenage son who needed treatment. Hal was aware that his motive for seeing his father would have struck her—struck many people—as indecent.

"Who are *you*?" his dad asked him, the next day.

"Hal," he said, and added to make sure, "Your son?"

"Never heard of you."

Then his father turned away, as if from someone seeking to sell him something he would never buy in a million years.

Good, Hal thought.

The two of them were equally ornery. At forty-six, Hal had become even more like the old man, as if a drug he'd taken decades ago had finally taken effect or worn off. They were so alike now, in fact, that they loathed each other: it was more than the dislike that had been there from his birth.

"How was he?" Jalene asked when she returned.

Hal shook his head, to imply, hopeless. Before she could express sympathy, he asked:

"And your son?"

"What?" She'd already forgotten about the therapist (or had fibbed in the first place, Hal thought). "Oh, he's fine."

"I'm glad!"

Jalene smiled, again expressing what a swell fellow she considered him. Hal did not say how he felt that his dad no longer knew him: unbelievably relieved.

For a day, Hal celebrated that he would never have to see his father again. When his euphoria faded, he sensed simply staying away would be unseemly. This made him—and he was not proud of it—annoyed.

"I'm not proud of it," he told his friend.

Robin was Hal's oldest pal (he'd known him since high school) and probably his only one left, given how he had alienated all others. Hal didn't know why Robin had stuck by him. Maybe because, unlike Hal, he had remained kind and nonjudgmental? Or, as an actor, was he simply interested in and observant of everyone?

"Won't you miss him?" Robin asked at their monthly lunch.

"I just feel guilt, honestly. And even that might simply be instinctive, I'm not sure."

"I don't believe it."

Robin thought the best of him or merely remembered when he *had* been better. Hal marveled at how angry Robin *wasn't*, how bitter he *hadn't* become, even though his promising career had been derailed by the pandemic and never recovered. Robin did odd, non-acting gigs and always politely yet proudly denied Hal's offers of loans.

"Believe it," Hal said. "It's true."

Robin shook his head, adamantly and, as ever, didn't order a second drink when Hal did.

"I can see it in your eyes," Robin said.

This stopped Hal, his hand fiddling in the air for the waiter. Did Robin really perceive Hal's true spirit? No: *that* Hal was dead, he thought. It made him remember the lack of recognition in his father's eyes.

"Let me run something by you," Hal said, adding his first to his second finger to signal "two more," before assuring his pal about to protest, "This will be on me."

At last, Robin agreed that he would relieve Hal's burden. He would tell Hal's father that *he* was Hal. He didn't approve of being paid for it, though.

"Why not?" Hal asked, exasperated he would even have to.

"It's unseemly."

"It's helping *me*."

"No," Robin said. "Me."

In the end, Robin stopped arguing. As an Uber pulled up to take Hal away, Robin suddenly hugged him. To convey his gratitude? Or to absorb Hal in a way before he went to work as him? Hal didn't know, but he had to struggle a bit to get free.

"So. How'd it go?"

After the first day, Hal hadn't heard anything so—more interested than he was willing to admit—he'd called Robin.

"Um, fine." The actor seemed to choose his words carefully.

"Dad didn't know you, right?"

"Right."

"Good."

"At the beginning."

"What do you mean?"

Robin paused, as if again trying to decide how to proceed. "I…often observe little gestures and actions." The actor began warming to his subject. "That's how I build a character. And something came back to me about you, from a long time ago."

"What was that?"

"It was the way you once kindly moved a wayward hair from my forehead. It was right before I was about to meet someone, a woman, maybe, on a first date. I reached out and did that to your dad. With what little hair he has left."

"And what did *he* do?"

"He looked into my eyes, smiled, and said, 'Hal?'"

Hal kept quiet long enough that Robin said…

"Hal?"

…just as his father had. This jolted Hal into replying:

"Was he confused?"

"Not for long."

"Then what?"

"Relieved. Warm. Loving."

"Oh."

Hal said nothing more and Robin followed his lead. At last, the actor jumped in (getting used to being employed, Hal dismissively imagined, later):

"So, I'll keep going?"

"Yes. Sure. If you'd like," Hal said.

"I would. When should I…"

"When would you want to?"

"Friday?"

It was Wednesday. Hal thought when *he'd* visited, it had only been once a week. Okay, he thought, every ten days. Sometimes, every two weeks. Three weeks.

"Sounds good," Hal said.

"Great!"

"And how should I…I mean, is PayPal okay, or…"

"Sure." Robin sounded genuinely indifferent. "Whatever."

The next time, Hal called Jalene (whom he'd warned what would happen, hoping that her it's-only-a-job attitude might make it okay) and said…

"Just checking in. Robin came? That's the actor's name."

"He told me." Jalene was eating; he'd called her at home and at dinnertime. She seemed miffed he wouldn't have known she knew. "Actually, Robin asked me to call him 'Hal.' It was very something of him, he said. I can't remember the term."

"Very 'method'?"

"That's it."

Hal let it pass. "And how'd it go, all right?"

"Great." She chewed more heartily. "They watched tennis together. Sat side-by-side on the sofa. Had a great time."

"Tennis?"

Hal used to enjoy the sport, on court and on TV. His father had introduced him to it. He and Robin used to play together, once upon a time. That had been fun, he thought.

"Did he know Robin?" Hal asked. "My father?"

"Know him?"

"Recognize him."

"As him?"

"As me."

"Oh. Yes. Right away." She swallowed.

"Huh. Okay. Thanks."

Before hanging up, Jalene said something else, but her speech was still slurred.

"He even kish him."

Hal looked at his phone. Even kissed him? That couldn't have been right, he thought. That was impossible.

Hal decided to show up, unannounced, on Robin's "day off." Jalene looked at him with alarm, as if he were an intruder, maybe a menace. It was different from when she'd believed him a great guy. Then she calmed down.

"He's in there." She pointed to his dad's closed door.

"Asleep?"

"I don't know."

Jalene sounded withholding, not unsure. Hal began to gently knock, then thought better of it and pushed the door open, as if breaking it down.

Absently combing his sparse hair with his fingers, his father was slumped in a chair before the TV. A tennis match was playing. He stared at it with (Hal thought) longing, wistfulness, and nostalgia.

"Dad?"

The old man turned with agonized slowness and squinted at his guest. Hal was panting and—even though the apartment was air-conditioned—sweating.

"Who are *you*?" his father asked.

"Hal? Your son?"

"Never heard of you," he said and increased the volume.

Later, Hal called Robin and was annoyed that he was made to leave a message.

"Sorry I didn't get back," Robin said the next day, when he did.

"I bet." Hal was aware he sounded petulant. *He* wasn't so good an actor that he could conceal it, he thought, resentfully.

"Look," he blurted out, for he had no clear idea why he'd called or had intended to say, "I have to let you go."

"Sorry?"

"Not let you go. I mean, it's not *necessary* anymore. I don't need you to see my dad."

"Really? But he loves seeing me. Seeing you, I mean."

"Then mission accomplished."

"You sure?"

"Look, if you must know…I can't keep paying you."

This wasn't true—Hal could swing it. (He'd initially seen it as worth every penny.) *He* hadn't rehearsed his lines, as Robin did: He was improvising!

"I can lend you some," Robin said, "if you need it."

"What? No thanks!"

"Just let me know."

"Look—it's your funeral!"

Hal didn't know what else to say. He realized there was nothing he could do to stop him. Robin was out of his hands, like a person in the past.

Hal dropped by his father's apartment, but no one answered the doorbell. He was fumbling for his spare key as a man from next door came out into the hall. Hal had never seen him before. To be honest, he'd never noticed anyone in the building.

"They left," the man said.

"Who?"

"The ambulance people."

Before he could ask anything else, the man was gone, as if he'd only had two lines in this lousy movie of his life, Hal thought. Then he opened his father's door.

"Dad?"

The place was empty. After Hal reached the bedroom, he saw that the sheets had been removed and rolled up, as they might have been in a vacated hospital ward. Even the old, stained mattress pad had been peeled off and plopped at the foot.

Hal sat on the bed, stunned. He picked up the old landline phone to call Jalene, but it, too, was dead.

At his own home, he called the nurse's number but no one answered and there wasn't any voicemail. Hal did hear Robin's recorded voice, though, when he left a message.

"Let's meet at the usual place tomorrow?"

Hal had tried and failed not to sound plaintive. He received no call back.

He was relieved to find the actor already at their table when he arrived. Robin gave Hal a brief smile and, unlike Hal, begged off anything stronger than club soda.

"So," Hal said, because the two had stayed silent for too long. "When was the last time you saw him?"

"Who?"

"My *father*. Who else?"

"Oh. Just now. Before I came."

"What do you mean?"

Robin seemed preoccupied by a recent pleasant memory.

"We went to the park. It was Dad's first time out in months. It sure was fun. And a big step forward. For the two of us."

"What? No, but he's dead, he's...."

Hal stopped talking. Robin didn't seem to hear him, as if he were speaking from a great distance.

When they parted outside, it was Robin's car that arrived. Hal hugged him and then held on, as if trying to absorb himself but he couldn't, he couldn't, for the life of him.

Appropriate

It was a thud, not a ping. The automated salesman said it would be a ping, and that's why Lee chose it. Now she realized she should have gotten the chime, for it was by definition melodic and could not be twisted—as apparently could a ping—to mean a dull and monotonous thud, not dissimilar to an anvil striking stone.

Maybe Lee shouldn't have chosen the alert at all when she'd bought Millie's device. She'd bought one for herself, too, to get the mother-daughter discount, but it had been voided by the extra fee to make the alert "blind" and not "shared," sent only to Lee's device when an inappropriate image or idea appeared on Millie's. It made no sense to "share" the alert with the teenager receiving the image or idea, did it? So, the whole thing had been a wash, savings-wise.

Still, Lee had only a second of self-doubt about getting the alert. She felt it had been the right thing to do, meant she cared, wasn't being intrusive or controlling or a censor or any other negative interpretation. Lee thought of her own mother and how *she* had acted about the same issue. While Lee knew it was apples and oranges, a different world now, she believed her own behavior was a big improvement, ping or no ping.

Lee's mother, Sable, had been contradictory and confusing about what Lee could or couldn't see: her rules were weird. In those days, of course, consuming entertainment sometimes meant leaving the house, if there were enough people signed up to justify opening one of the last theaters left, now being used for other purposes (retail, religious, military). Sable teased that Lee was "old-fashioned" for occasionally wanting to see things on the outside, where a mother couldn't *completely* control her choices, Lee had suspected, with the bitter, worldly cynicism of the fifteen-year-old. Yet which narrative conventions and story tropes Sable made off-limits was unclear. Allowed: unjustly accused robot lovers on the run…virtual prostitutes seducing and killing virtual cops… sadistic space aliens eating the brains of humans. Forbidden: animals learning to speak and shoot guns…infants and the elderly body-switching…doomed, drug-addicted suburbanites having hypocritical love affairs.

Peculiarly, it was this last that most provoked Sable's prohibition. The situation had reached a head with the dropping of *Intimate*, the most talked-about deca-drama of its day. It was six hundred ten-minute episodes about infidelities, marriages, and murders in a gentrified development built on a town's collapsed downtown—not unlike the one to which Lee and her mother had moved after their neighborhood was flooded into extinction. (*Intimate* had two meanings, was both adjective and verb, meant familiar and to be suggestive, something much cited by automated critics.)

"But why not?" Lee had asked when Sable forbade her to see it.

"You know why," Sable answered, yet Lee did not.

Lee hadn't obeyed—she couldn't, not when all the kids were talking about *that* scene in the 266th episode of *Intimate*, in which people performed *that* act. You had to see it in person, with a full house; it wouldn't be as deliciously excruciating in the privacy of your home; it was the kind of phenomenon that occurred once a decade and defined an era, she mustn't miss it. So, Lee had lied that she was studying at her friend Frieda's and even turned off the GPS on her old device, primitive compared to today's models in that it *could* be turned off.

Lee sensed the tension in the giant, packed theater (which had been a roller rink the night before and would be a prison holding pen and botanical garden in the days ahead, all remaining public events using the one available place). She put on 3-D holographic glasses, adjusting them to maximum sharpness, so she could touch and be touched by the performers, even feel their breaths lightly blowing on her skin. When *that* scene began—and everyone knew which scene it was—there was utter silence in the enormous, adjustable space, all sounds (moaning, crying, begging, giggling, screaming, puckering up, blowing out) coming just from the wall-spanning screen.

And then…Lee thought it must have been her glasses, a glitch in their reception, that only she could see it. She saw *her*, saw Sable, her mother was in *that* scene, committing *that* act, playing a part or playing herself, Lee didn't know. She would never know for she would never mention it to her mother, who would never mention it to her; no one ever mentioned it, so only Lee could have seen it, maybe only imagined it. Right? ("Appropriate" also had two meanings: adjective and verb: suitable or proper and to take, often without permission.)

From then on, Lee never defied her mother and only saw what she deemed acceptable. She'd done so from incredulity and fear, having been shell-shocked by *that* scene, not from the belief that her mother had been right. She vowed to raise Millie differently, to be open and honest, to discuss why she could or couldn't see something, to share the decision as they shared this new device and the ping that would alert Lee when her daughter went astray, even if Millie would never know.

The ping—the thud—had been going the whole time, half-heeded by Lee, preoccupied by her past. Today, a reboot of *Intimate* was dropping on devices, since there were no more mass public events. It was animated, as all entertainment had become, humans replaced by creatures living (raccoons, ducks, bumblebees) and inanimate (robots, dishes, germs). *That* scene had been retained yet altered for the new less physical, sensual, and tactile world.

Lee was sure that this was what had appeared on Millie's device. The alert would let Lee see it first: another extra charge had given her an exclusive preview before its premiere for Millie.

She cut off the ping with a flick of her finger above a key, no contact needed any longer between digit and device. The screen below her bloomed like a bouquet (she had shelled out for the exploding flower feature, too). There, as Lee had anticipated—desired and feared—was *that* scene, re-imagined.

Alone, as rapt as the crowd years before, Lee squinted, then stared at this new, non-human version. It was part cartoon, part computerized photo, part some other technology Lee couldn't identify, which hadn't existed until this instant. Lee caught her breath. She swore she saw her mother again, an artist's or machine's rendering. Then she realized it wasn't Sable but herself, committing the same shocking, scandalous, awful, forbidden, thrilling act forever.

Chip

There were so many of them. For a second, one was isolated above Gil, as if frozen in the air, near enough for him to study. That's when he came to the realization.

It seemed unlikely, even absurd: this younger one was bigger than Gil. Yet Gil could have sworn that the kid was colored in a weird way, had a fringe that reminded him of… and then the others swarmed away and the kid flew with them, not too fast to keep Gil from following, using the kid's weird colors as a way to keep up, the colors a beacon, a light that led him on.

The colors reminded him of the boy's mother, if in fact she could have *been* his mother, which was the unlikely, even absurd part. While a green-brown fringe was common among females, they were unheard-of in males, and this was why Gil thought the boy might have been Sally's son, and so his own.

(Gil hadn't named her Sally; I did. I'm imagining what Gil thought as I imagined his name, because no one knows how or even *if* an insect thinks, let alone one as far down the food chain as Gil, who was a yellow-golden dung fly.)

Gil followed the younger, bigger, brightly colored dung fly, and the pursuit led him into the past, as if their beating wings had wiped away the present. There Gil had been moving after other flies, too, most of whom were now long dead, for their lifespans were only one or two months. Gil was nearing his own end, and he knew it—I imagine—and this made him curious, if not desperate, to know what offspring he might be leaving behind.

In this past flight, he had been acting from instinct and not curiosity, heading to the same place the younger fly was now, a dung pile left by a horse on a farm in upstate New York. As he approached it, Gil slowed, for he had seen who was waiting.

Many other males hovered above or had landed upon the steaming pile (pat? Pad? Whatever was the most common term. Chip? No, that meant dead, done, and dried-up. Chip off the old block! Gil's mind was wandering.) Most, if not all, were larger than Gil; he felt a familiar, seasonal fear start to fill his modest frame. Yet he could not turn back; he was propelled ahead by an imperative in himself: the only reason he existed? It gave him no pleasure, he felt just obligation— no, that was a choice—only *obedience*, as he directed himself down, down, down into the miasma of other flies.

Even though Gil was a diminutive model, his instinct to reproduce was no less enormous than males of larger size, so his challenge was greater than theirs and his chance of success much lower.

"Hey! Look who's here!"

That's what one fly would have yelled if he could have said something and not just buzzed, if he could even do that. In any case, alighting upon the field of feces (it looked as big as a field to him), Gil was immediately waylaid by a bully who identified him as a target easy to take down.

And take down Gil he did, jumping onto his back around which he wrapped with tentacle arms. Gil tried to wiggle free but this only encouraged his attacker to attach himself more tightly, making Gil unable to move, let alone fight back. Like a wrestler (the idea of which he was utterly ignorant), the larger fly flipped Gil over so that he was splayed upon the rich, soft, and redolent surface, his belly exposed, his limbs twitching pointlessly. Then, his tentacles more and more like human arms, the bully picked up Gil (evoking another comparison of which flies were utterly ignorant, as might be most young readers) like a bartender booting a customer by the collar out the door onto the street, he tossed the smaller specimen a small distance from where they were.

Gil's tiny body twirled in the air until he was right-side up when he landed and skidded to a stop on the dung. As his eyes cleared, he saw before him a familiar, chaotic tableau: an orgy on the sponge of the cow's plop, scores of male flies quivering and twitching into females from behind, occasionally with enough force to push the females forward. This mass was depositing its genetic material upon another kind of deposit, creating a new crop of creatures on a bigger creature's crap.

Of course, Gil would not be taking part: he was prevented by the physical fact of his size. It was an unmistakable sign of weakness to his brawny competitors, who had not been outfitted with any sense of fairness and bore only the most basic and brutal need to copulate, if that's what you could even call what they were doing. Yet Gil knew he had not been singled out. Even those who had been chosen by females for this function (and who was choosing and not merely being forced was unclear) had to fight to finish. They were often interrupted in mid-act, not by a courteous tap to "cut in" but by other aggressors' smash-and-grabs to replace the rutting flies with themselves, sometimes accidentally and fatally puncturing the female in the process. Elsewhere, the fierce need to fornicate made males mount other males—whether from confusion or indiscriminate desire—which caused still more fights, the dung hosting a donnybrook of dominance no matter where one looked.

Gil looked everywhere, for he was desperate to escape. He'd given up getting anything out of or putting anything *into* this barbaric breeding ground. Yet he had to schedule his move for the few seconds when he wasn't being scouted for attack, when males were distracted by the arrival of new females. In this brief window, he soon took off from the battlefield, leaving the sights, sounds, and smells of desire, defecation, and death below.

For a while, he merely floated, relieved to be alive. And "floated" was appropriate, as this was officially what he was called now—a floater, a male displaced from the main mating arena of fresh cow dung. He never would get used to being this, yet it was his lot in life. Gil had settled for mating instead on everything from slime molds to fungi to sewage, with whatever females would join him. This day, though, had been different. This day, having been made hungry by being harassed, jumped, and pummeled, Gil sensed the presence of food underneath him: a composting apple squashed flat upon the ground.

Gil descended upon it. He began nibbling tiny and tasty bits of petrifying and putrefying citrus. There were others near him who had had the same idea. Gil ignored them, so engaged was he by this opportunity, which was such a relief from his (and I wish he could have appreciated this pun) recent fruitless pursuit. Only when he'd had his fill did he look up and, with a start, notice someone beside him.

It was a female, bigger (of course) than Gil. She had the green-brown fringe of her gender and was also duller overall than him. Still, the shifting midday sun did for her what her own nature could not: it illuminated her. She seemed to spray rays in all directions. She was—I decided—named Sally.

Gil assumed that Sally had come there for the same reason he had, to flee the oppressive atmosphere of the dung pile. While bigger males there may have had more generous testes that could dispense stronger sperm in Sally, they could also harm or kill her in their attempt to protect her from their competitors. Plus, there were so many on the dung that Sally had no ability or time to choose for herself. Gil perceived this in the way she now turned and offered herself to him.

He guessed that Sally had had many males on the dung before arriving at the apple and knew what she did not want. Her last lover, to use the word loosely, would provide eighty percent of her offspring. She had decided it would be Gil, whose small stature suggested he would be gentle, a trait she wished desperately to pass on.

Gil pushed the lower part of his abdomen against the higher part of hers. His front legs rested on her wings; his middle legs hung alongside while his rear legs gripped the base of Sally's body. She let it happen, wanted it to happen: they were linked by their contempt for cruelty, their taste for tenderness, their sense that the other was the same, their need to create more creatures like them, to further the feeling of love in the world.

Sally pressed herself into Gil to accept the pumping release of his sperm, the way to add this information to others. The event lasted two hours, the sweet scent of rotting seeds in the air all along. They knew nothing about time, adding and eliminating life as they loved each other, or whatever they were doing that day on an apple instead of on dung.

Afterwards, there were no exhales or after-glow, cigarettes or glasses of wine, not even an acknowledgment of the experience or of the other's existence. The last act Gil performed in Sally's presence was to fly away, while she went to deposit a compassionate and fertilized future into the sinking and stinking spoilage underneath.

Now Gil trailed who he felt *was* that future. The fact that the boy brandished Sally's green-brown fringe convinced him that the two had succeeded in their unspoken scheme to merge male and female, to make gentler the next generation. (Swiftly reproducing life forms, like flies, evolved more swiftly. Even months could bring big changes: the future was never far away!) The larger, younger male dung fly was on the edge of escaping yet compelled by an irrational parental instinct and the excitement it instilled, Gil kept pace.

"Wait!" Gil cried or buzzed but the other couldn't hear. Maybe Gil didn't want him to wait, wanted the positive progress he had put in place to occur, even or especially without him.

The younger fly did slow then but not in response to Gil's yelled request. Below, he had spied the dung pile where he and so many others were headed. Gil brought up the rear of their convoy and began to sink, never losing sight of his and Sally's beautiful son. (I've named the kid Chip.)

The pile was almost identical to the one he and Sally had bolted from months before. It was the same riot of male flies impatiently waiting to conquer females and combat and kill their competition. The sky was so smeared with them that Gil could barely see as he descended.

He saw enough to see the sun shine on and brighten his son's fringe as it had once done Sally's. As if the light was a ladder, Gil rappelled it toward the barely moving body of his boy. Chip had started to stop in the packed crowd of assaulting suitors.

Chip approached a male fly about to mount a female. Then Gil's and Sally's son—in fact it was not their son but my figment of a male fly that was existent always, this aspect of males, anyway, always existent—brutally dropped and disabled the other. Chip impaled him with his tentacles, spraying the other's insides all over himself, covering and camouflaging his mere fluke of a female fringe, hiding it as cops flip their badges to hide their identities when they're about to beat someone. After Gil cried out for him to stop, Chip turned and saw him. Then he began to advance on the old runt who would be no opponent for him at all.

Simultaneously

Pavel placed the salad on the table.

"It's the one you like," he called.

"Thanks," his mother called back from the kitchen. He'd let himself in with his key. "I'm hungry. What is it again?"

"Turkey."

"You cooked a turkey?"

"It's a chef's salad from the diner."

"Oh!" As if this changed everything. "Thanks."

His mother made no move to enter the main room.

"Why don't you eat it?" he said.

"Eat what?"

"The turkey."

"You cooked a turkey?"

"No, it's the chef's salad from the diner."

"Oh! Thanks. Not right now."

"Why not? It's the one you like."

"I'm not hungry."

Pavel had no time to reply before someone else's hunger was made clear. His mother's small dog, Bolo, had started jumping up and down to reach the plastic bowl, the tin foil on which he was starting to remove.

"Down, girl," he said.

"What's that?" his mother said.

"I was talking to the dog." Pavel began making baby talk to distract Bolo from the dinner. "Come on! Who's a good girl? Are you a good girl?"

"Yes," his mother said.

"What's that?" Bolo had been barking.

"I said I'm good. Everything's fine."

Too busy to reply, Pavel was following Bolo, who had assumed the hunkered down, I'm-ready-to-play position before running off. He pursued her for a few feet and then was stopped by a patch of the animal's feces, around which Bolo had expertly maneuvered. He saw that it wasn't the only example of her excrement on his mother's once well-maintained and now utterly mangy carpet. (Pavel's parents had lived in this dark one-bedroom in midtown for decades, and it was where he had been raised.)

"Mom?"

"Yes?"

"You haven't been taking her out?"

"Who?"

After Pavel stopped, he turned and saw something else piled upon her dinner table: mail that had gone unopened for weeks. A rent notice was on top, as if stranded there and screaming for help.

"Mom?"

"Yes?"

"That money I send you…"

"What's that?"

"Could you come out here, please?"

There was a pause during which their battle of wills was fought in silence. Eventually, his mother capitulated and entered the living room. She was completely unkempt, in a stained dress she never removed even to sleep, and her once-lustrous white hair was the color of the cloudiest sky of her life. She was shifted strangely to one side, so that part of her face was obscured.

"What's wrong with your face?"

"What's what with my what?"

"Turn towards me."

With a weird and hammy smile—tada!—his mother did so, revealing a bruise that covered half her head, as purple as one on a boxer who'd been beaten to death. Her part-pirouette sent a spray of vodka smell Pavel's way.

"I hit my head on the bathroom door when I opened it," she said.

"I think it was the floor, but forget it."

"What do you mean?"

"I think it's time to bring someone in full-time."

Dabbed by old lipstick as if by blood, his mother's lips began to tremble and her voice grew clogged.

"I don't want that."

"What *do* you want?"

"I want you to move back in."

Pavel knew that, while addressing him, his mother meant his father, to whom he bore a strong resemblance. She had become a serious alcoholic since he died of cancer two years ago.

"You know I can't do that," he said.

"Oh, no? Why not?" As if he were a lying child.

"Besides the fact that I'm forty-five, married, with children of my own?" Why did he bother? "Look, I'm sorry Dad died, but…"

Hit by this blast of truth, his mother rocked a bit backwards, her eyes widening and then narrowing as if having no choice but to allow it in. Then she threw up both her hands in a show of exasperation.

"Everything was going so well!" she cried.

She spoke as if she had never known that death might be a possibility for her husband or herself, had been kept by him from all unpalatable facts of life: this had been their understanding, their arrangement, their marriage. The dog shit on the floor, the empties, the black eye—they were the inevitable results of its unraveling. She would never accept it.

"We're going to have to bring someone in," he said, for the umpteenth time. Then he saw his mother obdurately shake her swollen head no.

"I'll be back tomorrow," he said, and the dog barked, as if protesting or cheering he couldn't tell which: animals were more opaque than people.

Pavel knew he'd keep providing food and plastic poop bags, paying the bills, trying to protect her, as if his father had done with more success. Alone in the elevator going down, he said aloud, "I wish she'd died first," and realized that his lips could be read in the silent security feed. He mouthed, "Just kidding," even though of course he was not.

Pavel didn't bring a chef's salad to his next stop: he knew it wasn't necessary. Here, instead of keeping an arm's length from anyone, he was drawn immediately into an embrace, which took him an effort to end.

"It's okay," he said. "It's okay, Dad."

"Hungry?" his father asked.

"No, thanks. I'm fine."

"You sure? It'll only go to waste. Come and put the feedbag on!"

Pavel had to admit the spread looked inviting when he entered the living room. He saw stuffed sandwiches, sides such as dripping coleslaw, and desserts from cookies to cakes decoratively arranged on a shiny oak table. The drapes had been parted and the big picture window opened, revealing a fifteenth-story view of a harbor and its flotilla of pleasure boats and yachts. The place inside was no less impressive: an immaculately kept and cozy penthouse with steel furniture in the latest style.

"Good, huh?" his father asked about the juicy corned beef, but Pavel's mouth was too full to answer.

His father had one arm firmly around Pavel's shoulders, as if this was all he needed to secure his son's place in the world. His confidence hadn't changed, had merely been transferred to his new home, which he had already filled with fancy new possessions and his big personality.

"Why don't you say hello?"

His father pointed at the open door to a bedroom, beyond which lurked the person to whom he referred. Pavel perceived that this was what he owed after having partaken of his father's good will. He nodded and more whispered than called:

"Hi, Astrid!"

After a second, there was a weak female reply, almost inaudible when a breeze blew past the boats and passed through the room.

"She's tired today," his father said.

Pavel remembered that Astrid had been tired the last time he visited, too. As before, he heard dance music from a device playing in the bedroom. The volume had been lowered; now it was raised.

"She has a lot of pep," his father said, "being so young. And that can tucker her out. Better to already be old and exhausted, right? Saves a step."

Pavel could see strain starting to show beneath the old man's eyes. Astrid was his new wife; he was thirty years her senior. He'd married her two years after his mother died of cancer.

Discomfited, Pavel looked away, taking in unfamiliar objects.

"Is that lamp new?" he asked.

"Yep," his father said. "So are the rug, the wallpaper, and the tea service. The gal's got taste, right?"

Pavel could only flee his father's emphatic positivity so far. At last, his eyes landed on three suitcases, still unpacked, in a corner.

"Someone moving out?" he asked, trying not to sound hopeful.

"Moving in," his father said.

The bags were made of craggy, virile leather.

"Astrid's pal Milo is a lifeguard at the club"—the place at which he and Astrid met. "He was fired for performing a too-saucy tired swimmer's carry. So now he's crashing here."

Pavel could have sworn he heard a muted masculine growl added to the female murmur beyond the bedroom door, right before it was kicked definitively shut.

"Milo's a great guy," his father said. "I hope he'll get on his feet soon."

His own double meaning seemed lost on him.

"Until then," Pavel asked, "it's your treat?"

His father seemed relieved at having this acknowledged. Playing to type, he protruded his lower lip in imitation of an infant and theatrically pulled out his empty front pocket. Then, uncomfortable even being comically candid, he yanked a packed wallet from his back pocket and waved it around.

"Nah, everything's fine," his father said. "Nothing to see here. Move along!"

Slowly, Pavel opened his own wallet. He removed the cash he had on hand—a lot, for it was Christmas tipping time—and forced it into his father's palm. To his shock, the old man took it, giving him a quick glance of gratitude. Then he turned away and watched the boats list in the breeze.

"If only I could have done more to save your mom," he said.

He still felt responsible for everything, as he had for better or worse in their marriage. "Some things are out of our hands, Dad," Pavel said to no avail.

Astrid had accepted the old man's protection in order to lean on him financially. His mother had done so emotionally, and his father had returned the favor. Some arrangements better suited our psyches. Now his father was the one made helpless.

If only he'd died first, Pavel thought but of course couldn't say.

Pavel's last stop was his first real one. It was a fancy hotel not far from his parents' apartment, the lobby restaurant of which had been their favorite brunch spot. ("The hollandaise sauce is heaven," or something, either his mother or his father always said.)

The concierge accompanied Pavel to the fifth floor. There, taking one and then two turns in the hall, he saw paramedics and police.

Over the phone, Pavel had been told that the chambermaid found them. His parents had taken an overdose of Nembutal and were holding hands on a double bed where they had died simultaneously. Simultaneously, on his drive there, Pavel had felt relief and grief, like his parents, in control and utterly at sea. The three had another thing in common: they had all seen the future.

Gift

There was a lot left unsaid, but that's how it had always been with them. Dill (short for Dillingham) and his sister understood each other better than anyone else. They were fraternal twins and so shared only fifty percent of their DNA. Yet they had always felt closer, identical even, as absurd as that sounded.

"What will you have?" he asked, after scanning the menu with his phone.

"Salmon burger," Della said.

"Same."

They were silent for a while before going back to small talk, the banality of which they knew meant something different, something deeper, unknown to others, as had the gibberish they'd giggled and chattered to each other as babies in their cribs.

They were actually talking about his illness, Dill was aware. It was a condition so rare, deadly, and untreatable that his doctor had called it a "hit-and-run" when she (kind of compassionately and kind of giving up on him) revealed his diagnosis.

At first, Dill had been afraid Della might have it, too. Then he remembered the fifty percent part and was relieved. It was weird to think that she would live longer than him (they were only thirty-five). They'd always done everything together. Dying, it turned out, would be different.

"I can barely see the print, anyway," he shrugged, pointing at the menu. He was referring to the oddly dim lighting in the diner, which had been Della's choice (she was usually laissez-faire where they met each week for lunch). He noticed Della was tilted slightly to the side, favoring the darkest part of the place, like a movie actress who knew her best angle. This was strange, too, since she had never been vain, not in the least.

The food came, and their chit-chat continued as they chewed, each triviality hiding the shock, rage, and fear they felt about his disease. The whole time, Dill saw that his sister stayed swiveled and even tried to tug the brim of her page boy haircut farther down upon her brow.

Suddenly, the candles on a nearby birthday cake illuminated their corner before being blown out. The applause seemed heartless, given what Dill had seen.

His sister had purple bruises beginning on her temple and ending near her neck. There was no point in pretending they had been caused by anything other than a human hand or that her brother hadn't perceived them.

"Jesus," he said.

"All right," Della said, to encourage him not to start up.

"How'd *that* happen?"

"It doesn't matter."

"No? Why not?"

Della didn't answer immediately. Then she was direct, both to shock and shut him down and because it was what she believed.

"It's nothing," she said, "compared to what you're going through."

That was as specific as their conversation got. The ensuing innocuous palaver was more strained, given what came before. They parted without another word about things that mattered, the place of talk taken as ever by their type of telepathy.

Dill knew that Della's new boyfriend was a fortyish doctor, so he had naively assumed the man to be civilized. *This* guy was physically sadistic? Dill located the email where she'd first casually mentioned him and it did not take long for Dill to find him in the flesh.

Dr. Sydney Porter looked civilized, too: balding, bearded, heavyset. He wasn't Della's type at all, which was young, lean, blondish, frankly moronic, and disposable male ditzes—Dill usually dated dumbbells, too, and never for very long. Obviously, Porter thought faster and moved slower than her usual dates. Emerging from his midtown office, he moved slowly enough, in fact, for Dill to follow him in a car he had rented for the day and this purpose.

Dill followed until Porter took a turn on the town's main drag (in truth, this was already the sixth time Dill had scouted him, the sixth day he'd driven this way). By now, he knew that Porter always parked on a side street. To save money on a lot or a monthly pass? He seemed cheap—look at his suit, Dill thought. Porter always left work after the sun had set and the block was lit by just one streetlamp, for the town was cheap, too. Then, being boringly obedient, he would wait for a green light to cross, even if the avenue was empty.

If Dill's doctor had called his disease a "hit-and-run," now Dill would become his disease before it became him, like dirt growing over where a tree had been. Even if he was caught, who cared? How long would his punishment—his life—last? It would be worth it. He would do it for Della.

In the crosswalk, Dill caught Porter in his brights like that blot isolated on his X-ray. (So, was Porter the disease or was he?) Then he overrode the car's automatic commands and hit the gas.

Della called their next lunch a day early, the day after the "accident" occurred. Dill didn't expect her to be *glad* that she had been mysteriously freed of her abuser by an unknown assailant. Yet he wasn't prepared for her actual response.

It took Della so long to stop crying about Porter's death that the waitress approached and then tiptoed away. She began to speak once or twice, but it was impossible through her tears.

Dill wondered if he had picked the wrong culprit. Or was this a new and unique way they now were different? Had Della, for the first time—ill-advisedly, self-destructively—fallen in love? Soon her sobs subsided enough for her to say.

Today there was no avoidance, prevarication, or reading of minds. Della confessed that Dr. Sydney Porter was a major medical researcher: she had done some research of him on her own. His focus was Dill's incurable disease, the eradication of which he had been steadily approaching. He was a brilliant but troubled person.

"Sydney worked best if he was defeating someone else. It seemed to give him strength," she said. "He didn't want to be the same as others, he wanted to be more powerful—that's how insecure he was. He made more progress on the illness the more he hurt me. I let it happen. How long could the punishment last? I did it for you. And now look what's happened. Now you'll never be cured."

At this, Della recommenced crying—so hard it was like a storm you feared would break your fortified windows and drown you in your home. Color escaping his face, Dill moved a shaking hand across the table onto hers. So much had been said today but Dill knew one thing would stay silent: the twins would keep on loving each other, even if it killed them.

Empathy

Who was he now? Ragnar had been able to be anyone, everyone. That was his trademark, his talent, his "brand," as the obnoxious new parlance went. He was the author who could evoke all kinds of individuals—men, women and children, every race, creed and color, as the idiotic old parlance went. He could even get inside the heads of animals: Kiernan the Corgi was his most beloved creation. "We Are All Kiernan," the translated French headline hollered; that was how completely he brought that dog to life. "Empathy" was his middle name, the internet bellowed. He was Ragnar "Empathy" McMullens, which was shortened to "Empath" McMullens, and then to "Path," his nickname narrowing until he was a straight line that led into the souls of others.

Well, not any more he wasn't. That's what had been decided by…who? Some vague, invisible institution of the air, the "zeitgeist," as the annoying timeless parlance went. It said that Ragnar had no right to be anyone other than himself, that the souls of others were theirs alone to express and were unavailable to artists who, without even asking, had absconded with them. His latest book advance had been returned, his contract ended before it began, his career over after decades without his having failed, with him only overstepping boundaries he had not even known existed.

So, who was he now? No one. Ragnar had so completely identified with other creatures that he had subsumed himself in them, like sugar that merged with and melted in their tea, and no longer existed as a soul. Even a ghost had once been alive. He was not even an apparition, but a non-entity, as big a nobody as dumb old death. How could he express *himself* when there was no one there to be?

"Ragnar McMullens?"

The woman handing out name tags didn't wait before she stripped off the backing and pressed it to his chest, as if awarding him the medal of his identity. For the first time in years, he was attending a family function—a memorial service, no less—for, disallowed to work, he was unoccupied and felt and suffered from his solitude (Ragnar had seen two marriages end due to his very absence of presence and, at forty, had no kids).

She'd spelled his first name with an "e," not an "a": Ragner.

"The N is silent," he said, puckishly, knowing that it left him at least on paper as "Rager," which amused him (though if she pronounced it "Rah-ger," that would kill the joke and mean nothing). This woman didn't answer and simply steered him to the reception room of the church (he'd purposely arrived too late to see the service) where she abandoned him to strangers. To virtual strangers—relatives he'd barely bumped into for decades, so engaged had he been with his work. The cousin in question, the corpse, to be exact, was someone with whom he'd grown up but hadn't known as an adult. He'd only been invited in a mass email.

Ragnar saw guests glance at his name tag and squint, trying to place him in their pasts—or their Kindle librar- ies, he dared flatter himself—and always come up blank. (They didn't even know Kiernan the Corgi? he wondered. Ragnar remembered that his family—both nuclear and extended—had been anti-intellectual, essentially illiterate, one reason he had fled.) He was left to awkwardly eat hors d'oeuvres—salmon and parsley on a cracker—biting down as if through the layers of the Earth, the crust to the core, to bury himself, then clapping the crumbs from his hands to deny *he* was dead and eavesdropping on those around him whispering…

"In the woods."

"What?"

"That's where she met him."

"Oh."

"It's a surprise. She seemed so…"

"Mousy?"

"Exactly."

"I guess you never know whose motor will run fast."

"The mother, too."

"You mean…"

"She's the angrier of the two."

"Interesting."

"Shh."

The two people—women in their forties—turned and caught Ragnar leaning in to glean their gossip, a cracker snapping in two between his fingers and both halves cascading to the carpet. They moved away after sneaking a peek at his name tag without recognition.

The women had continued a story being mentioned in low tones by other mourners. Using his retired storytelling skills, Ragnar pieced it together. A modest teenage girl in the family had been sneaking away during the pandemic to meet a local boy in the forest. Her parents had been appalled to find out, the mother (modest herself, Ragnar thought) reacting the most violently. The event had disturbed the dull equilibrium of his uninteresting clan, providing something exciting—alive!—to discuss during this celebration of death.

Soon, Ragnar saw that the philistine nincompoops, to whom he was barely related, were glancing to the side, to one corner. Ragnar zeroed in on who secured this spot, half-hidden in the near distance. He deduced it was the scandalous family, arguing in hisses: a gawky, coltish, about-to-be-beautiful teenage girl; her still stunning, much shorter mother, on the far side of forty; *her* once-handsome now bleary, paunchy and unattractively balding husband, who had beaten his wife in the race to reach fifty by two years.

Studying them, Ragnar suddenly felt sick. At first, he feared it was a nasty reaction to the possibly spoiled salmon. Then he recalled that he had barely eaten the hors d'oeuvres and actually swallowed only one. The sensation was something else: an internal purging of his empathy, so strong that it sent it springing out of him, boinging into the blue.

His empathy landed behind the eyes of the teenage girl, Belinda (he immediately knew her name). She was bolting from beside her "mom and dad," Hethe and Bruce, angrily exiting the church on newly long legs that took her at shocking speed into the parking lot. There, from her tiny disco bag, she retrieved a phone she had refused to relinquish to Bruce and Hethe. Chopping her thumbs on it with the skill of a Gyuto knife artist, she called Weyworth, the boy whom she had met (and kissed and touched and felt and loved) in the forest, both still obediently and erotically masked.

After a few sweaty seconds (it was hella hot, as the kids *used* to say, with no trees on the asphalt and no cloud in the sky), she held Weyworth in her hands. A skinny ginger, he was in a large square, out of breath as if he'd run there to see her, as he had every time to the woods.

"I thought you'd never call," he panted.

"I couldn't get away," Ragnar as Belinda said. He was bemused that the boy wouldn't have known why. "It *is* a memorial service, you know."

This meant nothing to Weyworth, who kept uttering words as hot as he looked, as wet as his upper lip, where perspiration was puddling (Belinda felt much cooler, though outside: He seemed to be in his bedroom, in his bedroom *closet*, it looked like).

"Your hunger makes me feel both fond and queasy," Ragnar as Belinda said.

Weyworth had been in mid-promise of pleasures yet to come. "Sorry?"

"It's endearing in some ways and a little arousing but horrifying in others," he as she told him. "Your need."

A painting moving in his frame, Weyworth blinked for a while.

"Well, that's a little condescending," he said.

"No, it's not," Belinda, who was Ragnar, said. "I said you were endearing."

"That's what's condescending. Like from a distance, a great height. Don't you…feel the same way? You seemed to in the forest."

His voice broke, piercingly, and Ragnar thought he saw the phone screen crack. It might as well have, for his empathy squeezed inside it, then inside Weyworth. Ragnar spelunked the funky cave of the closet, where Weyworth had hidden spunk-encrusted shorts from his mother (or his maid? The closet wood was walnut). Then he attached himself to the boy's brain like a spider's web upon its wall.

Freed of Ragnar, Belinda belatedly perceived how Weyworth had criticized her. Super-sensitive and already on edge from her recent encounter with her "mom and dad," she burst into tears. The girl's hands trembling, her image shook on the screen the boy clutched, as if she were enduring an earthquake (which she was in a way, emotions being so explosive for one her age).

"I can't believe you'd say that to me," she said, through phlegm-soaked static. "It's so…mean," and the last word was barely audible.

Ragnar thought: *she'd* been the one unkind to Weyworth, or at least Ragnar had been, when he was her. Yet this wasn't what he as Weyworth said, which was…

"It's touching and funny to see all your emotions."

It took Belinda a second to reply, and her grip of the device steadied. "What?"

"There are so many emotions bursting out of you, Belinda. They'll never be as easily released again in your life. Your pain, your joy, your love are so lubricated. Enjoy them—now, now!"

As opposed to Weyworth, who had grown more animated in his virtual cell, Belinda appeared to ice over.

"That is very creepy," she said, sniffing back the last drop of emotions he'd mentioned.

"Well, I don't think so. High praise!"

"It's like something a pervert teacher would say, leaning over your shoulder in class, or something. What are you now, a strange, sick, forty-year-old man?"

This gave Ragnar as Weyworth pause, which he took, saying nothing.

"I think we shouldn't see each other for a while," Belinda said.

"*What?* After what we had this week?" Ragnar thought it was the right thing to say, but it was too late.

"Maybe my mom was right about us. Anyway, they're both here. Goodbye."

Belinda disappeared, replaced on his device by corporate logos multiplying and crawling like cockroaches across the screen. Then Ragnar himself disappeared from Weyworth, the boy starting to sob, too, Ragnar popped out toaster-style by his thin, shaking shoulders.

Belinda's parents did indeed stand behind her. Hethe's heavy makeup and Bruce's burgundy hair color were starting to shake, bake, and cake in the sun. Their daughter stalked off, literally and figuratively out of their hands.

"Well, there she goes," Bruce sighed, licking up a bead of his own salted water.

Ragnar's empathy now slid behind the wheel of Hethe, as it were, handed the keys to her cranium. She turned and took it out on her husband.

"What," Ragnar/Hethe said, "you're just going to stand there and accept this?"

"Belinda's a teenager," Bruce said, backing up a bit verbally. "You were once that age. We both were."

"You identify with her too much," Ragnar as Hethe blurted out. "You forgive her everything because you can't separate yourself. You can't grow up and be the parent. You're clutching at Belinda to keep young. That's not love, that's not fatherhood—that's pathetic!"

Bruce reeled a bit, unused to words this direct from Hethe, to any interpretations from her. Sweat popping and bubbling like boils on his pale brow, he waited to speak, long enough for Ragnar's empathy to jump on and into him, grabbing the reins of his runaway stagecoach.

"Well, at least I'm not so bitter about my youth," he/he said, "that I want to prevent my daughter from having a better one. You didn't have pleasure—you can't have pleasure—so why should Belinda? You're more of a jealous loon than someone's loving mother!"

Hethe was startled by this taut attack from her flabby husband. Steamed in more ways than one in the exposed and pitiless parking lot, she yelled:

"I just want her to be safe!"

"Well, I just want her to be free!"

Neither Bruce nor his handler Ragnar was prepared for Hethe's swinging her purse—which had a long enough leather strap to lasso—at his mouth, to shut it forever. The action sent Ragnar flying from Bruce like a flea off a spanked spaniel, far enough away that he couldn't catch the continuation of their marital exchange.

He landed blocks north on an actual spaniel, a King Charles, whom he made bark at and bite his obnoxious owner, now yanking him too hard by a leash clipped at the neck, when…

"It should be at my waist, you idiot!" he growled and snapped at the human, scared by the sudden savagery of his beloved twelve-year-old, Sweetstuff.

The dog was the last place Ragnar's empathy stopped before it returned to its host. Ragnar felt himself swallow it back down, emitting an uncomfortably loud burp once he'd accepted it.

He stood in the threshold of the church, front door open, half in and half out, artificial air cooling his behind, the world's natural furnace burning his face. He knew who he was now. His self was judgmental, harsh, insightful, maybe a bit nasty, but brilliant, and so beyond bland societal standards. Someone had died (uncle, cousin, whoever) but he had been reborn as Ragnar: Ragnar again existed.

Ragnar walked to the car he'd called, a Lyft or an Uber, either one soaring above others as he did now (from joy, not superiority). In the parking lot, he passed a family—father, mother, teenage girl—at their earthbound Audi, fighting amongst themselves, crying and castigating, calling each other new names as if knowing each other for the first time. Ragnar observed them, which is what he did so well. Before he forgot this whole experience, he felt for them. Then he entered the car and the next path of his brilliant career.

Repair

"How do you feel?"

Lex had asked the question so many times it had become rote. Yet today she yearned to know the answer, she couldn't explain why.

The boy (man, young man, guy in his twenties, Boone, who cared what she called him?) strained to lift his head from his pillow. His lean face, fair before, was now so pale as to be translucent, transparent, whatever was the right word, she wasn't thinking straight. Anyway, he looked saint-like, Lex thought.

"Better now," he rasped.

"Good," she said.

Lex didn't feel guilty, not very, anyway. They always printed the recommended dosage on the bottle. She'd even told him what it was when she gave it to him, as she always did, to prevent an overdose like this—not to prevent a lawsuit; the Somatic Co. always made each customer sign a release absolving them of guilt—to show she cared, to be compassionate. It was Boone's own fault if he hadn't read the bottle or read it wrong. Right? Yet how could she blame him? He appeared so innocent. It had just been an accident, like everything else.

Boone's original condition had been an accident, too, the reason Lex was sent to his apartment the day before. His slurred speech, facial paralysis, and foggy cognition had been the result of a TIA or Transient Ischemic Attack, caused by a temporary (and *accidental*) lack of blood flow to the brain. Boone had learned this after entering his symptoms into UDOC, which had automatically called Lex so she could come with her trusty bag of tricks, as she labeled the supplements she had been licensed (after an eight-day course) to administer to people.

"You're the Suppleplier?" Boone had asked yesterday or tried to ask through his half-frozen face, using her new job title. (It was a mistake, Lex thought, when Somatic invented the title, the "TM" annoying to always add above or beside it.) The rigidity of his lips had made Boone so vulnerable, so endearing—all right, so lovable—that she couldn't keep from smiling when she'd answered...

"Yes," and whimsically rattled the bottle maracas-style, causing Boone's (blue) eyes to squint, the best he could do at a smile, given his TIA.

"Thanks," Boone had tried to say, as she placed the bottle in his palm, their hands touching for an instant as his fingers folded over them—another accident, Lex thought? (Every medical condition was decreed an accident now, caused only by physical forces: "Out with the inner life!" was Somatic's slogan, blazoned onto Lex's uniform blouse, also with a TM, beside "Somatic Repair.")

Today, after his ordeal, Boone's face had improved. His mouth was free to move again, his eyelids not drooping, his speech steady. He was so white as to be purified and—the word came quickly to Lex now—beautiful. It turned out TIAs only lasted twenty-four hours. It hadn't been the supplements—they'd been pumped out of him—and that gave Lex pause.

Lex hadn't had to come, of course. Once Boone's landlady called the police who alerted UDOC and they sent a technician with the stomach pump, she'd only been cc'ed by Somatic as a courtesy, pending their (obligatory, she was sure) inquiry. She'd *wanted* to be there.

"It wasn't your fault," Boone whispered.

"I didn't think it was," she said. "That's not why I came."

He didn't reply to that, just embellished what he'd said. "It was my fault. I didn't listen."

"I was worried, that was why."

She waited but Boone made no such warm remark to this woman twice his age. Lex didn't take that as a signal to stop—or leave—she kept on asking him questions, as if the more she asked, the more likely he would answer.

"Isn't there anyone here to care for you?"

Boone shook his head, swallowing with difficulty.

"I just moved in," he said, his voice growing dimmer with each word like a light bulb flickering out, "from my parents' house."

In fact, when Lex turned to the nightstand to grab a glass of water to give him, she saw what she hadn't noticed before. Unopened boxes were lined up in the living room like children pining for porridge in an old fairy tale. Lying a few feet away in the bedroom of his tiny apartment, Boone hadn't made a move to open them. Despite his physical recovery, he was still paralyzed.

"Do you miss them?" she asked. "Your parents?"

"No." Boone picked up and pressed a remote lying inches away in his bed. "Listen to this."

A screen spanned the entire wall opposite. Turned on by Boone, its picture was impeccable but its sound low, no matter how many times he theatrically pressed the volume. Suddenly, it got deafening and startled Lex; then it became inaudible.

"It's broken?" Lex said.

"It's my dad," Boone croaked. "He always makes you lean in to listen when he's not yelling like a gull. Either way, it's always about him."

On "him," Boone pointed again at the screen with the clicker before flicking it disgustedly beneath the sheets.

"It's a Compliance," he said, before falling silent, Lex's true cue to go.

In her Somatic-branded Jeep going home, Lex considered the encounter. She hadn't known Boone was a believer in "Compliances," one in a growing group of young people convinced that whether broken or super-functional, their appliances—phones, consoles, microwaves—could contain the spirits and evince the personalities of people in their lives.

It was a concerning trend, Lex thought. But wasn't it the inevitable result of believing that physical illness was only organic in origin, caused by nothing more than internal malfunctions? Boone and other boys (and they were mostly boys) could acknowledge human psychology as long as it affected anything besides their own behavior? Right? Lex wondered: wasn't it *possible* that the whole mind-body thing she'd read rumors about online…wasn't it *possible* that leaving his family, growing up, in other words, had caused Boone such stress and guilt that he had suffered a TIA in the first place?

Well, Lex thought, shrugging, as she approached the home where she lived alone, she'd be out of a job if such suspicion of the Somatic method spread. Doubts like this dawned on her most often when dealing with pretty patients, she was aware of it now. She had always diverted herself with work, unending entertainments on many devices, and her duties looking after her elderly mother in a nearby nursing home.

Tonight, after she entered her studio apartment, Lex had a new video message from her mother's attendant. The old woman had taken a turn for the worse.

After two more than her usual nightly glass of wine, Lex fell asleep. She awoke at dawn with a strange feeling on her face.

Glancing in the bathroom mirror, she saw that half of her features had dripped away from the other half. She looked like the French bell ringer in the children's musical cartoon.

Lex typed the symptoms into UDOC. They yielded a cause different from Boone's: "Bell's Palsy, an acute peripheral and temporary facial palsy…cause unknown."

In this condition, it wasn't easy to swallow the supplements Lex prescribed for other people. Only by frantically mashing a few first into paste and then dust was Lex able to ingest them, licking them from her fingers and forearms, and then she needed a glass of orange-flavored water to kill the chalky taste.

Lex did not wish to see her mother like this. The old woman had always been impeccably turned out—even in the dementia ward—and had from the time Lex was little insisted she be the same. That her mother was, according to the attendant, currently unconscious made no difference. With a thumb, she dabbed up the last trace of supplement.

Not long after waking up, Lex fell asleep again. Twelve hours later, when she regained consciousness, her condition was unchanged, the supplements had done nothing, and her mother was dead.

Boone was still flat on his back in bed, yet he showed no signs at all of impairment. Empty paper food containers were strewn upon his quilt beside biodegradable utensils and steel straws. The boxes containing the evidence of his earlier life were still sealed, like ruins of an empire that might be reassembled at any moment. Garish splotches of pink spoiled the white purity of his cheeks and his stubble looked as if black bugs had died upon his chin. The screen across from him had been shattered, possibly by a tossed shoe.

"What are *you* doing back here?" he asked, with disbelief.

Lex couldn't answer right away, for one side of her mouth was see-sawed down. Then she tried, addressing Boone in a voice both rushed and hushed, apologizing for barging in, confessing that she'd been wrong all along, that they all had been wrong, the supplements were worthless, the causes of conditions sometimes lay elsewhere, in our hearts and their minds. Why be afraid to admit it? Why were they all so afraid? She was afraid no longer, and how about him?

Lex felt drops on her hands, which were palms up, as if she were begging him. She looked down and saw that it was saliva from her half-shuttered mouth: her water was breaking, her ice melting, she was being born in water or going under it for good. Lex realized that she had hoped Boone would find her as beautiful in this state as she found him. She raised her head and saw that he was parting his own lips, but only to laugh.

Lex drove the Jeep home, moans escaping from the prison of her mouth. She had feared it would be a mistake to go and should have listened to the self expressing doubt. Maybe Boone had been right. What did she know? Who said *she* was so smart?

Now there was a new voice in her ears—or was it the same old one? Her mother yelled at her for everything from how she'd looked to what she'd said. Then her mother moved out of her head and took hold of the wheel, becoming the wheel. Her car was a Compliance (*was* it an appliance? Wasn't it a vehicle? Anyway, it was a big ticket item). The wheel swiftly started to spin, leading Lex to the left, without her looking in the rearview. She was being pushed into the passing lane, starting to hear the honks of horrified drivers, anticipating an accident.

Unless she was doing it herself.

Her hands shaking, Lex gripped the wheel and started to steer the opposite way.

Entertaining

The apartment seemed different, Leylah didn't know why. Had she dreamed that something happened and she'd awakened and it turned out to be true? Had it been one of those really realistic dreams, hardly a dream at all, not weird in other words, mostly a memory, and so not deserving of the word "dream"? Leylah didn't know that, either.

It must have been about the memorial service for her father, which had been held a month before. Leylah's dad had been the paterfamilias, (though he wasn't Italian), the Big Daddy, in other words, an autocrat, or just the oldest male left in the family. His large house had been the center of festivities for her extended clan, the home for *everyone's* holidays. Now that he was gone—Leylah's mother predeceased him—his generation was gone, too: all that remained was Leylah's younger, less impressive crowd, with lower-paying jobs, fewer kids (Leylah had none), and less ebullient or just less imposing or overbearing personalities.

They had smaller homes, too: Leylah had no house at all, just an apartment. So, at the service, she'd wondered who would be throwing Thanksgiving this year and answered her own question: no one. As she'd kissed her cousin Cloris goodbye—a girl she'd grown up with and never liked yet had gotten used to knowing, you know?—Leylah sensed she might never see her or any of the others again, not like before, their meeting place (already on the market) having been made immaterial, just as her father had.

"See you soon," Cloris had said, in her arms.

"Of course, we will," Leylah blurted out, as if her cousin's words hadn't been a pleasantry but a pledge or a promise. Cloris reared back, surprised by her insistence, which had sounded defensive, even desperate, because, of course, Leylah hadn't believed it herself.

As the weeks went on (this was September), no one stepped forward to invite anyone for Thanksgiving. Leylah began to accept that this aspect of her life—the world of her youth, the warmth or whatever it was she felt among her relatives, even those she thought idiots—was over.

Then, one day, she thought differently. Why couldn't *she* throw Thanksgiving?

"Because," her husband, Leopold, said.

"Because why?"

Leopold just extended his arms, to say, look at this place.

Admittedly, they had only two rooms, living and bed, both small. Yet Leylah suspected Leopold had never liked her family gatherings and thought her feelings childish—not suspected, knew—and might secretly be relieved to have them as dead as her dad.

"That's why I'll never be a Socialist," he'd once remarked, pointing to an online political site. "I can't stand collectives. Whether it's a family or a theater company..." He was a struggling playwright. "...they're all prisons to me."

This might have shaken Leylah's new commitment to becoming a...was there such a person as a materfamilias? At her age? 40? Then she remembered that "entertaining" had two meanings, to consider and to fete. She could do one and then the other. Right?

Leopold complained bitterly when Leylah sent out invitations, conscientiously cleaned the apartment, and rented tables that would span or even overshoot its narrow space. She received more acceptances than she had anticipated, gratified others in her family had had the same need for comfort and community, which *she* would fulfill.

On the morning of Thanksgiving, Leylah awoke to find they had one less room. Their one-bedroom had become a studio.

"I had nothing to do with it!" Leopold yelled, as Leylah stared accusingly at him. "I'm just as surprised as you!"

Leylah didn't believe him, she couldn't explain why. All the stuff she'd stashed behind the closed door of the bedroom now was strewn across, piled in towers and stuffed in corners of the single dining area. That night, there was little room to walk, let alone eat.

At the end of the cramped and awful evening, her cousin Cloris hugged her goodbye like one leaving a terminal patient for the final time, her face turned away, her lips kissing the cranberry-scented air.

"It wasn't me!" Leopold yelled again as Leylah wept, breaking a dish she had meant to wash, before trying to sleep on a small, exposed square of the only room they had left.

That had been weeks ago, Leylah remembered, as she awoke from the dream or maybe just the memory. She realized why the place felt different: it was emptier. Leopold had moved out or been asked to move by her, or maybe a little bit of both.

Now Leylah looked around and realized she was luxuriously back in her old bed and that her bedroom had returned. She had slept in the nude (which she never did with Leopold, for he'd said, "let's maintain a little mystery"). She rose and went out into the living room. In a newly elongated hall, she passed a den that had not been there before. Then she saw a second bathroom which had never existed, either. She found she could easily eat in the kitchen, which had once barely fit a refrigerator.

Leylah stopped, a materfamilias but also an infant, for look what she was wearing, nothing. She considered: it was three weeks until Christmas. She could get out the invitations if she tried.

Einzelheit

The old man had been so inspiring, Lorna thought, as she got into the elevator. Despite his age—seventy? Eighty? At thirty-eight, to her, he just seemed *old*—he had such energy and positivity. He'd ignited his corner of the party, where people had gathered around him.

"If you want to do something, do it," he'd said. "It's later than you think—go for it!"

Sometimes Lorna felt so frozen, but this old man was self-confident, wise, or merely indifferent to what others thought. Blanchard, was that his name?

"Sorry," Lorna said, holding the door for a woman now rushing in. Lorna had just pushed "close," which was kind of embarrassing.

"It's okay," said the woman, about seventy herself and striking, with close-cropped snow-white hair and good (Italian?) shoes. Lorna recognized her as someone in the Blanchard gaggle—Rita, was that her name?

"Quite a guy," Lorna said, after a second, because the silence discomforted her. She'd read you could tell a person's character by how she responded to silence: in *her* case, it was with insecurity.

"Who?" the woman said.

"Blanchard. Was that his…"

"Oh. Yes. Right." There was more silence as the car continued to fall. This time, the woman ended it. "Don't fool yourself."

"What do you mean?" Lorna said.

"He's full of it. Not dynamic at all. Just delusional."

Lorna waited for her to go on. She couldn't just keep saying, "Really?" or whatever.

"He's broke, dependent, helpless. Did you see the younger man and woman he was with?"

Lorna hadn't but said she had.

"They're his stepson and daughter-in-law. They've had him declared incompetent. They're exploiting him, sponging off him, holding him captive. They don't let him out of their sights. 'Quite a guy'!"

The car seemed to sink into and bob up from the lobby floor, like a space capsule splashing into an ocean, and then Rita was gone.

Waiting for the subway, Lorna thought about the encounter, made sober and uneasy by it. As the train arrived, she recognized a man getting in with her. He'd been at the party too, was about her own age, lean, with attractively unruly blond hair and good (Italian?) glasses. He acknowledged her with a smile, then asked if she'd mind him sitting beside her; he was polite as well. Lorna said no, not at all. His name was Lee Bellows, and he was a cinematographer, which was ideal: Lorna was an unemployed documentary screenwriter. She told him about Blanchard and what Rita had said.

"She seemed really sharp," Lorna said. "Smart, you know? A smart cookie."

Lee nodded and didn't respond. Before Lorna could be disturbed by the silence, he said…

"Well, I don't know how smart she could be when she voted for…" and he named the far-left fringe candidate in the last election who'd siphoned off enough votes from the moderate candidate to elect the far-right fringe candidate.

"Really?" Lorna said.

"I'm afraid so."

"But that's such a crank thing to do."

"I agree."

Now it was Lorna's time not to speak, feeling confused and dismayed. Lee filled in the gap.

"It's like a camera move in a film," he said. "One that includes a detail that adds to and changes what you see. The Germans call it 'Einzelheit.'"

"Huh," Lorna said. "I've never heard that word, but you're right."

Lee said it was his stop, and they exchanged numbers before he left.

When Lorna got home, she looked at Lee's number, saved in her phone's address book. She hadn't had a date in months nor a real relationship in more than two years. Then she took off her mask and called her friend, Maya.

"He seemed really nice," she said. "And nice-looking, too. Good hair and shoes."

"What was his name again?"

"Lee Bellows."

"Bellows? Plural?"

"Yes."

"Oh. You didn't hear about him?"

"Hear what?"

"He once kidnapped a friend's child to get back film equipment he said they'd borrowed and never gave back. No one got hurt, the lenses or whatever were returned, and the friend didn't press charges."

Lorna made little "mm-mm" sounds until, rattled, she excused herself and hung up. Before she could fully process her friend's information, she heard a lapping noise.

Lorna turned and saw her tabby cat, Margarine (a rescue, once stand-offish, now loving). The animal was near her super, Primo, who lay on the floor, with a steak knife in his chest. If Lorna had told him once, she'd told him a million times, there was too little heat. She had hypothyroidism and was always cold.

The cat was licking his blood, which was sticky on the floor. Lorna had forgotten to feed her before leaving. Making a kissing sound, she got Margarine to follow her into the kitchen.

"Einzelheit," Lorna heard the cat say.

Reality

Raymond's hand fluttered in his palm, throbbed as if it were a baby bird with a madly beating heart. Nate was twenty-two, and he was shocked to see the blue veins beneath the old man's pock-marked skin. Next stop, his skeleton, he thought, and there would be no secrets left. Suddenly, he felt the fingers start to fold around his own.

"Listen to me," his father said, so hoarsely it was hard to hear.

"I'm trying to," Nate said.

"Don't do what I did."

"Which was what?" After all, his dad had done a lot of things.

"Don't know." What did he mean? Did he mean "I don't know" or something else? Nate's dad didn't elaborate, as if he held his truth to be self-evident.

Even dying, the old man was a prickly, dark, and comic person, an attitude which had rubbed off on Nate. Raymond had always been blunt, even brutal about himself, his constant struggles, and—he wasn't afraid to admit—many failures. He had employed scathing self-satire, with a dour and droll delivery, coming from a stiff and stony face. Nate was also following in his footsteps by being self-effacing and unemployed.

Now Raymond nodded at the newspaper on the night table, old-fashioned enough to still read the print version and ask Nate to chase one down for him on the days he visited, no easy feat. He indicated the front-page stories about the current trend in self-delusion, the believing of lies, how it was winning elections and altering other areas of life. Nate's father raised a shaky thumb to show that he approved.

"Don't know," he repeated.

Nate realized he meant: be ignorant, live in the dark, stay stupid about yourself; doing the opposite had done nothing for him. Ray reared up alongside Nate's left ear, and his son could smell something new coming off him. Death? That Ensure stuff? Nate couldn't tell.

"A fake smile is as good as a real one," his father whispered and explained why. (The old man had also been an amateur science buff, too lazy—by his own lights—to ever apply to med school.) A smile, Raymond said, real or not, made the brain release neurotransmitters, molecules that fought off stress, relieved pain, and reduced heart rates. This "Facial Feedback Hypothesis" had been posited as long ago as the early 1900s by William James, the brother of...and here was where Nate stopped listening and his father sank back into the sheets, each admitting his own limitations, which in Nate's case was a short attention span and in his father's a small amount of time to live, for these were the last words he ever spoke.

Nate looked down at him. His father's skin immediately became more sheer, silken over his insides. It must have been his imagination, for that wasn't how it worked, was it? Nate reached up and tried to close the old man's eyes (Ray stared, as if—as usual—he saw everything too clearly) but it wasn't like it was in the movies and was too hard to do. Nate picked up the hand which had finally freed his own and held it, to perceive no pulse, for that's what they did in movies, too. Then tears poured like incontinent piss from his eyes.

Nate made himself smile, bigger and bigger, straining the sides of his mouth. He hoped his father had been right and he would feel better, even if the smile wasn't real.

"How do you feel?"

"Fine."

Nate felt fingers press on his wrist, checking the pulse.

"I'll say."

"Sorry?" This was an enthusiastic young doctor, examining him for a new job, and Nate wasn't used to him.

"You're in great shape."

"Well, if you already knew, why ask?"

The doctor shrugged, taken aback by Nate's snotty tone. "Reflex. And speaking of reflexes…" He went on to praise Nate's crack physical responses, the low numbers in his bodily network, the general robustness of his health. The gauges and tests that decided these things got results quickly now—they'd been improved in the five years since Raymond's death—you didn't have to wait weeks or whatever.

"You don't know the half of it," Nate was cocky enough to say about his condition.

Yet how *would* the doctor know? A check-up couldn't go *that* deep inside Nate's brain and glands, couldn't reveal how the pumping of neurotransmitters—dopamine, serotonin, endorphins—had been bathing him in positivity, as if from a faucet turned on by Nate's continual fake smiling. His father had been right: Nate's acne-scarred skin had cleared up, his hair (starting to thin when he was nineteen) had been replenished, his potency (never impressive) much improved. Had he even gotten taller? It felt like it, especially as Nate glanced down at the doctor, stoop-shouldered at twenty-seven, pointing at a TV screen mounted on a wall and always on.

"Will you look at those clowns?" the doc said.

He meant people taking willful ignorance to a new level, repeating lies "proving" the nonexistence of a currently rampaging and deadly disease. He didn't know, as Nate and Raymond did, that they might be made younger, stronger, and maybe even taller by believing it.

Lying on a table, Nate directed his bare bum at the doctor, and not just because he'd been requested to do so. The next exam would go even farther inside him, yet he knew it would reveal nothing. Nate felt himself being thrillingly filled up by sedatives, as if by more falsehoods.

When he opened his eyes, Nate was submerged in water. He bobbed to the top of a huge infinity pool, the whole Earth on his level. In the distance, he'd heard a bell, which had brought him to the surface. Now there was only silence. It must have been a ringing in his ears, which was odd since nothing was ever wrong with him. In fact, anyone who saw Nate spring from the deep end onto the imported tiles would have believed the man in a Speedo was half his age of forty and did nothing in his life but work out.

Of course, Nate did much more. The enormous mansion he entered, followed by falling water forming a filmy cape, was irrefutable evidence. In recent years, Nate had bought the company he had once been examined to join, and that had been the beginning of his global empire. It had been fueled by fake smiles but also by pleasing fabrications he paid employees to tell him, which had swelled not just his chest and buttocks but his bank accounts. He emulated all those on Earth, now overwhelmed everywhere by myth.

Yet Nate's achievements had come at the price of painful solitude. He employed women to fib that they loved him or loved sleeping with him, and it felt as good to hear as if they'd been honest. Yet he never asked any to stay overnight, let alone live with him. More and more, he dreamed of having something deeper with someone, and he was doing so now, thinking about a woman he'd met that morning. Nate had offered her a job and she'd turned him down, an unusual occurrence, given the unprecedentedly high salaries he could afford. Nate had seen something in her face when she said no: What?

Nate looked down. Chlorinated liquid had pooled at his feet on the marble floor of his giant living room. Someone else would mop it up. Then Nate recalled that his robot cleaning person was being repaired, and he was alone in the house.

He heard the bell again.

It was—had been all along—the front door. Nate walked to answer it, tickled by the opportunity, as privileged people are by taking actions of which everyone else is sick and tired (doing dishes, raising children, working).

The woman who refused him was there.

She was small and nondescript, slightly older than Nate or maybe just not packed in and preserved by lies. The only thing more direct than her stare was her attitude.

"I'm Aletheia Tsitsipas," she said. "I'm sure you remember." Then she entered without asking.

Nate didn't wonder how she'd found his address or over-ridden his vast security system. He realized what had been in her face that morning: she had known or at least seen through him.

"It was why I couldn't take the job," she said. Whether this knowledge made her ineligible or would simply have been unseemly was unstated.

Before her, Nate felt naked even though nominally dressed. She looked him up and down, not with appreciation—or not just—to confirm what he was and what must be done to him. Done *for* him, for this was the kind of person Aletheia was.

"It'll be for your own good," she said.

Suddenly, Nate knew that the years of loneliness had taken their toll: it was time, he decided, for something new.

"Yes," he said. "Please. Tell me the truth."

Aletheia advanced farther and did. She offered him facts about himself, researched and intuited, with the conviction he would be helped if not saved by hearing them.

"…lazy…crass…barely talented…insensitive…grating…morally repellent…"

She did not stop coming forward. The intensity of her expression plus her proximity made Nate back away. As he did, beads of moisture bounced from his well-muscled chest onto Aletheia's breasts and with a stab made sheer parts of her blouse, exposing her lacy flowered bra. The encounter seemed intimate, sexual, even if chaste.

"Don't stop," Nate said. "Please. Keep going."

Reversing, Nate slipped on drops he'd deposited behind him. He fell onto the cold stone, where he curled as if occupying less space would make him fetal and reborn. Aletheia loomed over him and rained down more reality, sure it would cause him to flourish and flower and not be drowned.

Yet, lying there, Nate found that his father was still right. Hormones and chemicals like cortisone and adrenaline began to irrigate his insides. Dopamine, serotonin, and norepinephrine rampaged unregulated, as a rebellion, to over-correct and protect him. All the work of what hadn't been true was undone. His biceps softened, his loud white teeth went quietly gray; the length and girth of his penis were returned—as if they'd always been on loan—to better lovers. Clumps of Nate's head and chest hair littered the marble underneath him.

Aletheia stopped, stunned, before the weak, twitching, and misshapen pile of Nate. She was aghast at the result of her having revealed what was true.

Nate made a great effort to lift the head flapping on the slight stalk of his neck. His face was as wan as Raymond's at the end. Then he parted his lips from his few remaining teeth and smiled.

"Is it real?" Aletheia asked, excited and confused.

"What do *you* think?" Nate said, with his final breath.

Redemption

"Horse trading," "pony up," "two-horse race"…so many of the old guy's expressions were animal or equine. Was this the way he saw himself, as sub or unhuman? Or maybe Kingston was just slathering on the country boy routine as thick as his white head of hair, his "thatch" of hair a better way to put it because it was more rural, more Huck Finn, or however the cornpone saw himself.

Could Kingston actually *be* this stupid, Crater wondered? He was a senator, after all. Of course, that could just mean he was cunning, ruthless, and obnoxious. Crater bet Kingston hadn't read half as much as *he* had in jail, where he'd finally gotten into reading (he'd barely cracked a spine—a book's spine—as a boy).

If you had told Crater when he *was* a kid—or an adult, for that matter—one day he'd be sitting opposite and nego-tiating with an old Southern senator, he would have said, get outta here, or just kicked you in the ass, that's the kind of miscreant he'd been. He'd committed no major crimes, just mischief—another old hat word, like "thatch"—petty larceny, pickpocketing, shoplifting, and the like. Road rage was what had landed Crater in jail, that was the funny part; he'd gotten away with all the rest. He'd been put away for impatience, really, for selfishness and immaturity, because he couldn't stand to be stuck in traffic one minute more and had gotten out and told the guy one car ahead of him so, then bashed the poor guy's window in with a brick before trying to stand and dance on his hood and sliding off, since the surface was too slick and Crater too drunk to stay upright. It hadn't been the other guy's fault; he'd just been stuck, too, and being adult about it, unlike Crater, who'd at long last gotten what he deserved and made to (at long last) grow up.

His sentence had been to serve weekend jail time, plus community service—picking up trash in a park—and seeing a social worker. Ramona had taken such a liking to him that (even though Crater fantasized about her, for she was a fine maybe fifty-year-old and he wasn't that much younger and open-minded about age—anyway, forget it, she couldn't have cared less about him in that way, liked women, it turned out) she'd put his name in for the program, the new one begun by the government.

And Crater had been *chosen*, that was the amazing thing. They'd read his application and decided he deserved it. The whole idea of the program was to give guys like him—selfish, incorrigible cock-ups—a chance to have the responsibility, authority, and dignity they'd long been denied, to "expand the pool," as they put it, of who could be leaders in the country, for a minute to give a poor excuse for a person like him power.

Crater was shocked by the happy look on Ramona's face when she heard. Who'd ever been happy for him, his mother, father, ex-wife? Nobody. For the first time, he'd felt proud: a new emotion, almost better than any drug he'd taken or sex he'd had. It made Crater want to do a good job in the post he'd been granted, a better job than he'd ever done at anything.

President of the United States, after all, was a big deal. Crater would only be President for a week while the actual president rested (Crater had never voted, wasn't registered, he didn't think, hadn't checked and couldn't remember, for what would have been the point, let's be honest, for a guy like him?). The week it happened was by good or bad luck budget negotiation time, and temporary President Crater had decided to do it personally, not leave it to some boring old budget director, as everyone assumed he would. That's how he came to be across the table now from corny and hirsute (a jail word) Senator Kingston. He was an infuriating fellow in the actual president's party or the other party, Crater couldn't remember, considered a "tough customer" and "hard nut to crack." Crater had dismissed the "working group," a crappy crowd of earnest and boring people, to go mano a mano with him.

"In the saddle," "champing at the bit," "win, place or show"—Kingston was still at it, the old annoyance. Was it to show he was a gambler, a daredevil, someone who would "go the distance" (one more) for his needy constituents, as he called them? They weren't constituents, Crater knew, but high rollers, big contributors, fat cats. That's to whom Kingston wanted the budget dough to go, for that's where it *always* went in this country, pushed into the pockets, stuffed down the bras, and spilled on the palms of the privileged. It was always a windfall for the wealthy, a stipend for the selfish, for the rest of their lousy lives!

Well, not under seven-day President Crater, it wouldn't be. Now that he'd been given the gig, he'd gotten religion— not real religion, that bored the fudge out of him. Crater wanted a payback, a make-good, a redistribution of wealth to compensate for this country's crimes and his own stupid life of not caring about anybody besides himself.

Senator Kingston didn't believe he was sincere, thought there was a catch, that Crater had an angle. Corrupt people couldn't comprehend everyone wasn't like them, their cynicism a way not to see themselves, this assumption an avenue to avoid their own guilt. At last, Kingston agreed to Crater's demands because he bet the funds would be flung at those not needing them, that Crater was as big a crook as him—right? As they parted ways, the senator even slapped the back of his new pal, President For a Week.

Months later, Crater wondered what Kingston would have said to see the government's gift finally being distributed, going where it would do the most good. He waited, anxious to witness the look on the recipient's face.

He knew she wouldn't be as little as the last time he saw her, which was a few years earlier, he couldn't remember how many. He wasn't thinking straight or being responsible then. When she showed up, Crater saw that his daughter, June, was six or seven years old. (His ex-wife had dropped her off and driven away, yelling, "Have her back at five—don't be your usual awful, selfish self!")

Then Crater stared as little June was diverted from staring at *him*—slightly scared, for he was a virtual stranger—to what the government had bought and he had brought for her. He'd gotten the idea while haggling with Kingston, and it had been a brainstorm, if he had to say so himself.

The pony had a big blue bow around her neck, like the great gift she was. She'd come special delivery from Saudi, the finest nag in the world. It would make up for all his years of neglect. Who was the selfish one *now*, Crater wanted to know?!

"Daddy!" June cried, thrilled. After hugging it and hugging it, she said, "I can't wait to show my friends. Can they ride her, too, Daddy? Can they?"

The new statesman and benefactor thought for a second. Then, growing into the change in his life…

"No," Crater said. "That would be wrong."

Nucleus

It wasn't the fact that she was going away; she had gone away many summers during college. And even though Amos always had a panicky feeling as soon as she left for overseas or another state—the sense that his daughter had slipped his hand while crossing the street—he always got over it, always had, anyway, by willfully forgetting or becoming fatalistic, by thinking, she was on her own now, he could not help her anymore, goodbye, good luck. But this was different; he was surprised by how different it was, and he didn't like it, didn't like what it said about him.

But what did it say, exactly? That he was shaken Randa was going on a trip to Bolivia with her college singing group and in the company of another girl, a girl who was more than her friend, who was her lover? Or would be by the time they got to Bolivia or after they had been in Bolivia for a while, that it was only a matter of time, in other words, if it hadn't happened already and it probably had, who was he kidding, besides himself?

It wasn't that Amos disapproved, because he didn't, didn't care about it in a moral way, morality had nothing to do with it, he was totally open-minded. For instance, at a work retreat last summer, he had been come onto quite openly by Shem Cutler from marketing, the completely bald guy who looked like a linebacker, with the big muscles, and Amos had just been flattered, amused that he was still young enough (at forty-four!) to be asked to be someone's prison bitch, instead of being "Pops" on the cell block, the guy who divvies up the cigarettes, keeps a pet mouse, and dies of a heart attack during the break-out. (And he only thought of prison because, well, Shem was big enough to be sort of scary in his form-fitting suits, so he looked like he could be, you know, kind of a convict, even though he was the gentlest guy—anyway, never mind, it didn't matter, it was just a joke.)

It wasn't any of that. Maybe it would have been the same if she were going away with a boy, which Randa never had, as far as he knew, though he had no idea what she'd been up to at school and didn't want to know (if his own experiences during those years were any indication, watch out!). But, no, he had to admit, even if it was so last century and only to himself (and even then he felt sheepish as if God could hear his thoughts, which he used to actually believe as a child) that it *was* different because it made Randa different from him and so feel further away, further even than her growing up had made her, as if she had actually *moved* to another country now, one that was hard to reach, so that he would not in a sense be seeing her as much anymore, which made him melancholy, as if a little love had leaked out of his life. It was corny to conceive of it that way, but that's how it made him feel, lonely, even lonelier than he usually did, for he was aware that he was lonely as a rule and always had been, and Randa had made him feel less so the second she was born.

Amos would have felt even worse if he hadn't seen how Sheila was reacting. He didn't ask her, not right away, instead he just *observed* how she was taking it and interpreted it. It was risky, but it didn't feel right to just *blurt out* the question, especially since he felt so uneasy about his own response (and by himself, forget with his wife). Still, he saw it in Sheila, a sort of forced smile when he discreetly mentioned it, as if she hadn't known this about her daughter—hadn't known since she was nine, as parents always said they did—and so this meant that Sheila felt she had failed, had not been as close or as good a friend to Randa as she'd supposed.

"Maybe it's a phase," Sheila said. "Though it doesn't have to be. I only meant…"

"I know what you meant."

Sheila nodded, relieved that Amos understood, that she didn't have to say she wasn't a bigot or anything, that they just had a similar sense of distance—was that it?— from their daughter now. The whole house seemed larger, as if it were a hotel or little inn that they ran and not a home, a place where other people only stayed briefly, you saw them at breakfast and that was it, you never really got to know them. And Randa was their only child.

"We'll get used to it," Sheila said, trying to be pragmatic and not so emotional, which wasn't easy for her.

"Sure."

"Though the girl she's going with…Ashley?"

"Amy."

"Amy. From the picture she sent…"—This was how they'd learned about it, in an email—"she seems a little, well, sloppy, doesn't she?"

Amos was noncommittal, suspecting that Sheila was being critical of this girl because she couldn't judge Randa: it was taboo or would expose too much about herself. He hoped that Sheila would stop after the one comment, but as the week went on, she kept going, becoming more and more judgmental about this Amy—whose name she had "not known" intentionally, he figured—finding fault in every aspect of her from the one small photo that was their only evidence of her existence, like a detective trying to crack a case from a single clue and assuming way too much. Randa would be gone for a month, and Amos was not looking for-ward to hearing this the whole time, but he kept his mouth shut (if there was one thing he had learned in marriage, it was when to do that; he was proud of that, other people never learned) and let her get it out of her system.

But that didn't mean he wasn't relieved when he got the phone call.

At first, it didn't quite sink in who the woman calling was. It was only what she wanted that appealed to him, which was to come see them and, he hoped, interrupt Sheila's unceasing sniping about this Amy, as well as enliven their newly and loudly quiet house. (Most of their friends in the suburb were gone for August and so unavailable for a dinner party, cook-out, or game night.) It was only after Amos hung up and explained to Sheila who it had been that it suddenly occurred to him how surprised, even shocked, he was by it.

"It was the donor," he said, inhaling as if to grab back and swallow down the word and the woman with it.

Sheila just stared at him, as if he had expressed a particularly crass vulgarity for no reason at all, was showing signs of early Alzheimer's or something,

"What did you say?" she asked in a tone which would have been a prelude to a punishment had he been a child and not a middle-aged man.

"The donor. Yolanda Bloom."

Sheila looked away then, as if slapped by the words, as if they were punishing *her*.

They had always known it was possible that they might hear from the donor. Though it had been controversial at the time, the government had made the names available to all who entered the program, when the transfers—*mitochondrial?* Amos always had trouble saying the word—began to be more common and the modifications more acceptable. And even though the donor was only providing a tiny amount of *mitochondrial* DNA—the part of Sheila's that was defective—it meant that there had always been three people involved, three parents in a sense, and they had known that. (And how fair was it that this small part of DNA was also the most powerful? Sheila asked, in tears, before they agreed to the procedure. Not fair, but life wasn't fair, Amos told her, comforting neither of them, but not knowing what else to say.) Yet though they knew it was possible, they never thought it would actually *happen*, her contacting them, her coming there, Sheila pointing out that the woman—Yolanda whatever; she had folded over the letter as soon as she saw the name—would have too much pride to track down her, what was it, 0.2% of her DNA? So now, while Sheila tried to stay even-keeled, it took an effort.

"Well, what does she *want?*" she asked, turning back, paler than when she'd turned away, as if the air had wiped off a layer of her pigmentation in the two turns, and she should have just stayed still.

"To meet Randa," Amos said, his own discomfort making him stammer a little (he hadn't since childhood).

"Did you tell her she isn't here?" And Sheila made it sound as if she meant, "Did you tell her she was an idiot?"

"Yes," Amos replied. "And then she said she wanted to meet *us.*"

For a weirdly long time, Sheila made an exasperated face. "I can't believe it."

Amos didn't answer. He didn't know why he always had to smooth the edges for Sheila when he himself was not all that *okay* with them. But that was their relationship, their arrangement. Every marriage was one, at least emotionally: Sheila openly expressed her upset and anxiety while he buried his own, ashamed of feeling them. It worked, it seemed to have worked, anyway, for more than twenty years.

Then Sheila nodded, very slowly, and Amos was reminded of an oil rig going into the Earth, finding something valuable and reemerging, except that Sheila went the opposite way, up and *then* down, so the analogy made no sense. "Tell her she can come," she said.

"What? Really?"

"Yes."

"But…"

"Please." She softened her tone, perhaps remembering to be reasonable and that she wasn't in this alone and was glad of it. "I mean, if it's okay with you."

Amos was silent, implying that it was, and that the exchange was over. He didn't admit that he had already told Yolanda yes, again secretly knowing when to keep things to himself.

She arrived that Friday night. Yolanda seemed attractive and engaging, but it was hard to tell, because she cried so much during dinner, which made her face puffy and red. She was about forty-five with a trim build and shoulder-length blonde hair tied—youthfully, like a teenager—in a ponytail.

In between mouthfuls of food (Sheila had made her special chicken with sweet potatoes—delicious) and helpless glugs of tears, Amos was able to piece together her tale. During the summer, she rented condos in the last seaside town in Maine. In winter, she produced stage reviews of punk rock era songs that toured senior citizen centers in Florida. Her partner in these businesses, who was also her long-time lover, had recently abandoned her, and when Yolanda examined their finances, she discovered there had been secret pilferage the entire time, which had now left her with nearly nothing.

"I feel so lost, that's why I came," she said, "I couldn't tell you over the phone," and this sentence was completely in the clear, for she was only drinking wine now, having finished eating and at least for a second stopped crying, the way a storm subsides but you can't relax and leave your umbrella at home, because it's been on and off all day. Once dessert was served, Yolanda became much calmer and ate it like someone even younger, intently and charmingly, like a child. Soon she grew loose and amusing, making profane remarks that were as funny as they were rude, which was a rarity these days, Amos thought. She listened politely as Amos and Sheila described *their* jobs (he was a lawyer for a company that made flood gates; she did P.R. for a group designing underground malls), though stifled a yawn here and there, again in an amusingly kid-like way.

As Amos watched her, he didn't believe she had come there for money; it was just a hunch, a snap judgment. She seemed to be genuinely seeking solace unselfconsciously from vaguely yet crucially connected strangers. Still, when he caught Sheila's eye as he rose to clear the plates, he knew that their exchange of glances had nothing to do with that (Sheila had probably never considered that Yolanda could be some kind of—what was the old word?—grifter). Instead, it was about the fact that Yolanda's partner had been named Becky and was a woman.

As he washed the dishes, Amos listened through the swinging kitchen doors as the women continued to talk. He picked up Randa's name many times now (the girl had hardly been mentioned during dinner, as if Yolanda had needed to finish her explosion of distress before anyone was allowed to even broach the subject, as if—and this was a completely corny way to put it, Amos knew, but whatever—their daughter was a rainbow that required a storm to introduce it). Amos was slightly hurt that they had only started to talk about her once he'd left the room; his diffidence might have misled them that he didn't care. (Surely Sheila knew that wasn't true: he would be miserable if after all these years that were so. No, it wasn't that. Maybe she just thought that women could talk in ways they couldn't if a man were around, especially since Yolanda was the way she was and Randa was...you know, that the little amount of DNA had been definitive). He wondered: Should the government have *allowed* them to know her name? Amos discounted the question, wasn't thinking straight, had drunk so much his hand without the sponge slipped and he only saved a plate by chance.

He waited for a break in their conversation so he might re-enter the room, but the talk never subsided long enough for it not to be awkward. He noticed that Yolanda began to cry a few more times, usually just as he was about to step through the swinging doors. He heard glasses being set down more often and more shakily on the table and then he, too, took another snootful from an aging bottle he found in the fridge. At last, he only peeked in long enough to give a little I'm-going-to-bed wave.

He saw that Sheila's eyes were red, as well, as if she had been actively commiserating with Yolanda or even sharing her own sorrows, though which ones Amos didn't know. Used tissues were scattered across the table like bits of rubble from their building's collapse.

"Oh, are you going to bed?" Sheila asked, fuzzily, even though he thought his wave had been more than clear.

"Yes," he said, almost inaudibly.

His wife weaved from her seat and hugged him, held him particularly close and long, whispering that Yolanda would be staying in Randa's room, for it wasn't decent to make her drive anywhere in this weather. It was pouring, he realized. He could hear it tapping on the air conditioner, like a crazed drummer.

Then Yolanda rose and hugged him too, more formally, and her wet face made his own face wet, as if she were smearing him with her sunscreen, protecting him like a parent; it felt nice. Or did it? He was so loaded, he didn't know. His mind was offering up ideas on its own, like the stewardess who lands the plane after the pilot passes out in that old movie; or—no, he knew—like his thoughts were being extracted as someone's DNA was by a cotton swab.

Hours later—how many?—Amos was awakened in his bed by silence. The rain had stopped performing, and the absence of its consistent sound had pulled him by the collar from unconsciousness. Even though it was a long time before the morning, he was already hungover; it had been years—how many?—since he'd drunk so much, and his head felt like an enormous red blister balanced upon his neck.

There was pain at the end of his legs, as well. As Amos sat up, he saw that someone was sitting on his feet. Sheila was at the bed's edge, facing away and looking out the door, as if listening to the whisper of light from the little night bulb in the hall bathroom. Feeling him move, she turned and her face—though still pink from all her weeping—was mostly white. She wore only a T-shirt and underpants, no bra.

"Is something," he tried to say through what felt like moss, dust, and twigs in his mouth, "wrong?"

"We were only touching each other," she said, her voice clogged by wine and tears. "Mostly touching, anyway. I don't know how I feel about it. It didn't feel bad, not physically. But that's not the point. I didn't want to be only one-third of her, that's all. Of Randa."

Amos fell slowly back as if knocked out by a cartoon boxer. The throb on his feet subsided as Sheila slid into bed beside him, or so he thought. Had she even been there in the first place and said what she'd said? He couldn't tell. Yet he didn't put his arm across her, as he usually—always—did.

In the morning, Amos knew that it was all true and had actually happened. He could tell from the way Sheila and Yolanda behaved. They were chatty yet maintained a distance from each other, sitting on separate sides of the table. Sheila seemed sheepish and kept directing what he thought were solicitous peeks at him. Plus, she had made her special whole wheat pancakes, which she rarely did. Or was it only because they had a guest?

She passed him his plate piled high, and Sheila's expression seemed to say, I'm sorry, you know why I did it with her, it wasn't infidelity, not really, I love you so much. Amos realized this was a lot to read into a person's features yet that's what he saw. His engorged head now felt the way he imagined mixed martial artists' do when their opponents gouge their eyes with fingers and hold onto their faces, at least in films. He suspected it might not have only been his hangover.

Yet the two women appeared to have no ill effects from the wine, perhaps had rubbed or kissed or sucked it out of each other the night before, Amos thought, surprising himself with his anger and the imagery it had conjured.

Yolanda's hair was down now, no more ponytail; she had become a grown woman, was no longer a girl. She began talking, disarmingly—chirpily, was that the word?—with the same amount of positive energy she had applied to negative things before. Overall, she appeared refreshed by events. Amos lost her words in the deafening clang and boom of syrup being poured and butter being spread—in his state, that's how they sounded to him—but he got the gist. She was grateful for their compassion and impressed and touched by the generosity and openness of their marriage, at least the one that Sheila must have told her they had last night.

"There's been such progress in the world," Yolanda said, with wonderment. "Not just in science, but in humanity, too."

Sheila looked at Amos after this and seemed to beseech him to stay silent, which for once at a crucial time in their marriage was not his inclination. Then she said Yolanda should stay until Randa came home, which seemed to be a very, very, long time from then.

That day after work, there was a drinks thing at a local bar. It was the kind which Amos always avoided, being an executive and so not liking to hobnob too much with those he supervised, believing it distorted working dynamics, encouraged a false familiarity, and impeded productivity. Or something. But tonight, he agreed to go, shocking his staff, and didn't call Sheila to say he'd be late.

He sat crushed between others at a long table in the back room of a deafening sports bar where screens in all corners showed ultra-violent electronic games. Amos felt like a guest at a baronial banquet after a primal battle or hunt, with backs being slapped, flagons of beer banged upon wood, and everyone swaying side to side in bawdy song. Still, for all their joviality, he sensed his crew felt restrained by his presence, was holding back from the true depths of their usual foul-mouthed fun, and had preferred it when he hadn't come.

After nursing just one beer—the idea of getting drunk again inconceivable (then why not do it every night? Why never *not* do it?)—Amos wandered down to a lower floor. It looked like the long, dank hall shrouded in shadows that might have been in the castle that hosted the banquet. Were there mounted swords and family crests on the walls? That's what he thought. Soon he emerged from the men's room, where he had peed into what appeared a trough in a stable-like expanse. He saw Shem Cutler, the big guy who'd, well, you know, made his interest known. He stood against a wall, chatting good-naturedly into a cell phone, and looked up and smiled distractedly at Amos. Like a superhero, Shem had burst from the suit that suffocated him and now wore only a T-shirt and jeans (no tights or shorts, but the effect was the same).

As Shem said a friendly "I love you" and snapped shut his phone, Amos approached him without a word. He thought of how colors mix to make new colors—blue and yellow made green—and how all those genes now mixed to make new parts of people, and how his anger at Sheila and his love for Randa and his desire not to die and his feeling of being utterly alone were mixing and making him feel something else, and then the two men were in each other's arms like the spirits of that castle, disappearing into the wood of the wall. Shem was as gentle as Amos thought—hoped—he might be, and they finished right before someone else, a co-worker, came down the stairs.

The next night, at dinner, there was little talk between Amos, Sheila, and Yolanda; plates were passed and food ingested virtually without interruption. Amos noticed that Sheila hadn't made any effort with the meal, had ordered in from the town's only Indian restaurant, the food of which had once given her diarrhea. Yolanda now wore a cunning little cap that hid her hair, so that she looked like a boy or, to be more exact, like someone else.

He surreptitiously studied the women's faces and saw no acknowledgement of one from the other, not even a shift of an eyeball or the hint of a smile. He imagined that one had been rebuffed but he didn't know which one or whether the rejection had been mutual. Had each merely known the other in the way she wanted and now had no desire for any additional involvement, as neither was taking seconds of the chicken tikka masala? At any rate, it seemed as if all three now ate on separate islands in outer space, an image that mixed the sea and sky, but Amos didn't mind, since both were vast areas of loneliness, one wet and one dry.

At bedtime, Amos said nothing, not because he was still angry at Sheila (and how angry had he *ever* been? He didn't know) but because he now had a whole new set of secrets to think about, which he stored in an apartment that had opened inside his brain and in which he lived alone. Sheila, who was usually so voluble even when about to sleep, would, once in a while, open her mouth, but then think better of it. Soon both were diverted by and bent forward to hear Yolanda mumbling animatedly in her sleep down the hall in Randa's room. But her actual words were indecipherable.

When Randa came home at week's end, Amos and Sheila introduced Yolanda as their old friend, since they had never revealed their participation in the program, feeling it was unnecessary or waiting for the right time which never came or not wanting to discomfort the girl, or some other reason they had never formulated. As was the wont of those her age, Randa seemed more interested in talking about herself, recounting her "amazing" trip and casually mentioning that during it she and her girlfriend, Amy, had become "kaput" and that she was now seeing a boy, Jamie, who wanted to work in home security after he graduated.

Sheila complained of a "horrible headache" and went to take a nap, shutting and locking the bedroom door. Amos sat by himself, staring out the window at two pigeons mating near the backyard bird feeder, wondering what two dirty city birds were doing out in the respectable suburbs. Then he was drawn from the strange sight by a sound.

It was the faint strains of a piano, coming from the den, where the instrument was kept and played only by Randa. He approached the door, closed but for a crack, and through it saw a slice of his daughter and the donor seated side by side on the stool. Yolanda was playing, and both were singing "The Rainbow Connection," a song written for puppets long ago.

Amos had always known that Randa had a beautiful voice, but he had had no knowledge of Yolanda's abilities, which were just as great if not more impressive. Tears entered his eyes like criminals creeping up on him from behind. Amos heard the two hit the same note, who was singing became indistinguishable, and it was as if this was what the elder had handed down to the younger, this and nothing else, this alone.

The Freelancer

Ranger noticed the other boy there, but he didn't think much of it. There were occasionally kids around the office, what was the big deal? Still, he didn't go out of his way to be the boy's pal or anything. Fuck that—why? He ignored him.

"I'm Trey," the kid said, having no choice but to volunteer the information and so seeming weak, like he couldn't take the silence. Ranger nodded, not saying his own name, being withholding, that's what they called it. He shook the hand offered quickly—not weakly, not like limply, firmly but fast, forcing the other boy to come up with the question.

"And your name is…?" Trey omitted the "what is" part, the "what is your name?" part, because it was too exposing, like a dog showing its belly. The kid made it a statement, an inquiry that needed an ending, because an actual question would have been enfeebling—a question mark was cowardly, Ranger thought, not really knowing why. Anyway, it was a smart move by Trey; because of it, he respected the new kid and responded.

"Ranger." He only had the one name, which pegged him as an orphan and dared the other boy—any boy, actually, but this one at this moment—to comment on it, which Trey didn't do. He just nodded and started out of the office, as if on an assignment, which bugged Ranger, for where did that leave *him*? Anyway, it could have been worse—another boy had once barked when he heard "Ranger," because it sounded like a dog's name, which bought the kid a beat-down, even though he thought it funny, he had to admit. In Ranger's world, everything was turf, how you walked, what you wore, even the words that came out of your mouth, and you had to protect that turf or concede it to someone else.

Now that Ranger thought about it, though, he realized Trey hadn't said *his* last name, either. So maybe *he* was an orphan, too, which made sense. Brenda preferred to hire them and send them out, felt they had less to lose—so was that what she'd done today, hired and sent out Trey instead of him? Why? What had he done wrong? Feeling angry, because it was less weak than feeling hurt, Ranger looked inside the office for the older woman who was his boss.

He found Brenda faced away, at her desk, talking on some new device Ranger couldn't afford and which only older, rich assholes had. Maybe when she wasn't looking, he'd take it; that would teach her for dicking him around and making him uneasy. He was her best boy. Not that he had to hear her say it, he wasn't weak like that, but Brenda ought to know Ranger knew his own worth and wouldn't put up with any shit.

Still, it took her forever to turn and see him and even then she just raised her eyebrows once, as if telling a delivery boy to wait, she'd be off in a second, and swiveled back the other way. Ranger wasn't used to this kind of treatment— who she did call day and night and know would accept any assignment? Him! Until recently, anyway, and not because of anything *he'd* done; he'd been more active and aggressive than ever, scouring sites for remains and such. But Brenda had let him go two whole days without a call and then, well, what was that Trey piece of shit doing there, anyway? What gave?

Brenda hung up—or got off or blinked off or whatever the hell you did with that device; Ranger would find out when he stole it. She turned and took him in with just the merest of glances, the way girls sometimes avoided his stares on the street—not all girls, don't fool yourself, plenty smiled at him, because he was good-looking, getting to be, anyway, fifteen was the start of a long and happy love life, he had no doubts at all in that department, believe me.

"What's up?" she asked, and her voice was flat.

"What do you mean?"

Ranger couldn't help asking. He hated that sound in her voice, that "get it over with" sound; he'd heard her use it on lots of people but never with him. Someone told him that Brenda had once been a big blogger, a gossip blogger, like she had posted stupid shit online about celebrities that people supposedly paid to read, subscribed to read, that was the way it had been said to him, paid every month to read, like money was something they couldn't wait to get rid of and so would use to buy any stupid old shit in order to have less of it, like money was poison in a snakebite you sucked in and spat out (he'd seen a TV show once about that over someone's shoulder on the train). Anyway, Brenda had done well at it until her site went under and she got fired and went to work for the Muth Co., where she sent out kids like him—not *like* him, *him*, until today!

"I mean," Brenda said, "what do you want?"

Now her tone had turned nasty instead of indifferent, which at least gave him something to work with. Ranger could fight, spent half his day doing it, in one way or another. So, he preferred Brenda being pissed at him; it was the ignoring, the back-turning, the giving up on him that he couldn't take. He answered with a similar air of anger, "To work—what else?"

Brenda looked confused. "Didn't I just give you something?"

Brenda had backslid into the dismissive territory that made him so unsettled. It was like she thought Trey had been *him* or hadn't cared *what* boy had gone out. Look, maybe she'd barely even met the other kid; maybe Trey had come around looking and got nothing from her, and that's why he had left. Ranger didn't want to deal with it any more, it was driving him crazy. So, he kept the edge in his voice, for at least it felt normal.

"No. What, you got a worm in your head?"

It wasn't witty, but it got his point across—he'd insulted Brenda, which meant he wasn't afraid of her, he was tough, which she'd always admired, for she was tough, too, and mean, and that's why they'd gotten along. (Ranger sensed that, as an adult, Brenda could always be meaner than him; he was fifteen and fifteen was, at this moment in this world, still not grown. Ranger may not have wanted to know the whole story yet, for—even though he longed for the sexual love that would mean he was a man—he'd have to leave a lot behind to grow up, and that made him afraid.)

"All right," Brenda sighed, and logged back onto her new device in a weird way, for she made no move but looked down. Was she trying to get rid of him? Ranger felt so shaky he was interpreting *everything* negatively, and he hated that. Anyway, she was about to throw him a job, and that was good.

"There was a nightclub opening last night," Brenda said, "and some sort-of stars were there." She scribbled on a piece of paper, an archaic custom she'd maintained, which gave her a timeless quality, as if she'd been sent there from the past or was maybe just aging slower than everyone else. Ranger thought she dressed like a younger woman, too, with her white buttoned-down shirt stuffed into her tight skirt and unbuttoned halfway down, exposing freckled breasts that Ranger didn't want to see but couldn't stop staring at, surprised he'd give a shit, since she was old enough to be his, what, great-grandmother, but knowing he had sex on the brain all day every day being fifteen, and also feeling bad because Brenda represented someone he wasn't *supposed* to desire, even though it was really all right, they weren't related—anyway, she tore it off, the piece of paper, and pushed it across her pristine black desk to him.

"That's the address."

After reading it: "Where is that?"

Brenda looked at him—what was the word?—witheringly, as if to say, do I have to do *everything*? This was not okay but at least not unprecedented. "Use your thing, for Chrissake."

She meant Ranger's pocket GPS gadget, the Beamer or whatever it was called, that got him to and from the blast sites—he'd forgotten for a second that he'd been issued one. Brenda had reminded him as if telling him to wipe his nose or do his homework, like—oh, why not come out and say it, stop being cute, he thought—the mother he didn't have and never had had.

"Okay," Ranger said apologetically, which was a departure, given his typical toughness. Maybe he'd intentionally forgotten about the Beamer, in order to be reminded by Brenda in that motherly way. In any case, he felt better, being berated by her. And that was enough for today, he thought, he'd gotten all he needed from her: a job. He turned away—but Brenda had already done the same thing first, which was weird.

Using the Beamer, Ranger took the train to the bus to the bus-train and back to the train-bus (or the Trus and the Brain, as other orphans called it). They let him out in the ass-end of town, at the site of the club Brenda had mentioned. It was now a skeletal and rickety frame helpless to protect a smoldering pile of wood, steel, and rocks. The explosion had taken place last night, and the minor celebrities in attendance had been from the music business, low level wankers who sang and danced. It was Ranger's job to get past the police and confiscate any items that might retain the DNA of these D-listers blown to bits, taking from the skin, intestines and other organs now scattered upon, dripping from, or wetly decorating the wreckage.

And this was his particular gift, his specialty, weaving in and out even when the cops told him to get lost, which they usually did. Ranger was almost like a rat (he didn't mind the comparison—rats were cool) that could shrink to slide under doors. Some cops compared him to smoke, wafting here and there before disappearing altogether. They said it with reluctant admiration, even though he fucked with their crime scenes. Was it that they didn't blame him entirely, because he was only a kid and a kid without any family or permanent home (he was currently sleeping on a cot in a disfigured building that once had been a church—whatever *that* was)? Or was it that there was a kind of weird connection between cops and crooks, because one in a way defined the other by being its opposite, the way you were defined by those you loved and hated? It was the closest Ranger had come to being known by anyone, except for Brenda, who hired him and sent him out.

"Hey!"

Today the cop had to yell—not because he was infuriated or even annoyed but to show his superiors that he was doing his job. In any case, Ranger whipped by him, went under the crime scene tapes, both actual and laser, to scoop up whatever pieces of furniture or floor might hold the most and least melted remains.

He had a plastic bag over his shoulder, like—what was the name of that bitch somebody mentioned used to exist?— Johnny Appleseed, but Ranger plucked and picked up, didn't put down and plant. He'd even worn his grooviest gloves, which were black leather but super-thin and close to the bone, like a second skin. Today his job was made easier by the sun, which shined on and made sparkle what the elderly called bling, vestiges of chains, bracelets, and earrings that drooped on door frames and toilet stalls, like in—again, who was the dude?—a Dali drawing, retaining aspects of beings. The sun was like his spy, working for *him*, because he was as big a badass as Earth! In his element, Ranger was now snapping off and stuffing down so fast, it was like he wasn't even stopping, like he was simply swallowing stuff, and you didn't stop to do that, did you? You did not.

Then Ranger *did* stop, screeched to a halt, that was the expression (he'd been taught to read by an old bum, but he had to break it off because of what the guy *really* wanted from him, and Ranger had been just a little boy, Jesus fucking Christ, whoever *he* was). He planted himself intentionally in anger the way someone else might mistakenly in mud.

Trey was there.

The little asshole from the office had gotten there ahead of him—*this* was where he'd been going when he left, he *had* been assigned by Brenda! Hadn't he? How else was he doing this now, yanking and placing bits of broken glass and black charred wood in *his* bag? It was a better bag, too: was that a new, more opaque plastic? Why didn't Ranger have that?

Ranger felt as if something was painfully hanging from and falling off his chest, like bricks breaking off a building on fire and landing on the ground. Suddenly, he wasn't so concerned about what he'd collected: it all seemed puny, second-rate, and superfluous (though he didn't know that word, only knew it was unnecessary). Even the money he would make was minor compared to the betrayal he was enduring; one thing could not compensate for the other; it was like being offered a blow job for a bullet wound, you know?

So, Ranger upended and emptied the bag, scattering the last evidence of those stupid failed singers and dancers—those human beings—making it unlikely they would ever be reborn. (He knew what the stuff was used for, what Brenda had been hired by the Muth Co. to hire *him* to do: retrieve and sell the DNA of near-nobodies, that was the best they could get these days, once their celebrity business collapsed; he wasn't stupid, just uneducated). Then he fled the scene, the crater that had been a club until just a few hours ago until some psycho with a religious or political reason had turned it and everyone in it and himself into just vestiges of themselves, suitable for scavenging by the likes of Ranger.

He retraced his steps and passed the first cop again—who didn't care, maybe had never cared—going in reverse, except nothing was rewound and came to life again. In fact, everything seemed deader than when he'd arrived; Ranger, too, felt less alive. (That wasn't true: because of Trey, tears were now jumping from his eyes as if escaping *his* burning building. His face was as hot as his heart, and that felt vital in a new and awful way.)

Wiping his cheeks, Ranger staggered from the site with no destination in mind, checking over his shoulder to see if Trey was still there. The bastard was, yanking shards from the shattered site and pressing them deep into his *better* bag, looking like a slave, picking cotton for his masters (Ranger had seen a music video about that once). Yeah, well, what did that make *him*? Ranger was simply competing to be the best scavenger, the finest stealer of cells, nothing for which a person should be proud, orphan or not.

But you know who was the worst? Brenda, because she was older and should have known better; she had sold celebrities before and was now selling losers when they were nothing but smears and slime and ripped ribbons of themselves. It was over, Ranger thought, he was through working for Brenda, picking up his pace as if actually on his way somewhere. Then, of course, he slowed and stopped because he was lost.

Ranger patted his back pocket, expecting to feel the familiar bulge of his Beamer, but he only touched his ass. The device had fallen out—or been swiped by the cop as Ranger sped past him, stranger things had happened. Instead of increasing them, desperation dried his tears now; and he looked every which way, with the world fiercely in focus. He saw closed stores and abandoned construction sites, no people—except, wait, there *was* a girl his own age standing on a far corner, tentatively raising her hand, either to swat something away or wave, he wasn't sure.

Ranger decided she was waving. He waved back, his fingers curled, seeming to scratch his nails on the chalkboard of a school he'd never attended. She smiled, which was his signal to cross; he was fifteen and still learning how it worked. She'd done her job, now he had one to do. It was a relief, and he did not wait, for she looked like the future and was not far away.

When he reached the other side, Ranger saw how small she was—everything about her was short, including her hair, which was in a buzzcut. In fact, she looked a little like *him*, only her face was softer; his was growing harder and darker every day, as if being cooked by the flame which was time since he turned twelve. She had on a T-shirt and khaki shorts, so she was like a ranger, too.

"Are you lost?" she asked.

"Yes."

He had just blurted out the answer, because who had ever asked him such a thing, ever asked him anything about how he felt? It was like that "maneuver" where they hold you hard and the chunk of food choking you popped out; she'd held him that way for a second.

"I lost my …" Suddenly, he couldn't remember the name of the stupid device; he tried to form its nebulous shape with his fingers, then gave up.

"Where are you trying to go?"

"I wasn't," he said, again ultra-honestly. "I was working."

"Where?"

He nodded at the ruins, which from across the street looked like a castle leveled centuries ago, an impossible place to do anything.

The girl was baffled. Then she shook her head, slowly and meaningfully, his occupation becoming clear. "Oh. Right."

"But I just quit," he said, half because of how she'd said it and half to see how it would sound. It sounded good, but a little unnerving, like the click when you close a door behind you without the key.

"What will you do now?" she asked, seeming to approve of his decision (or maybe he was just imposing this and she meant nothing by it and was simply making conversation; it wasn't clear; he hadn't talked much to girls).

Ranger shrugged. Coming from behind a cloud, the sun made him squint and seem even more uncertain. The sun was again giving him a hand as it had when it exposed the remains; now it said, show her how unsettled you are, go on, don't be embarrassed, she's here to help you—or so he imagined the sun said, still anthropomorphizing nature like a child.

"Where do you live?" She was grilling him—and literally, too, for the sun was extra hot, assisting him.

Ranger had been honest with her the whole time and would not stop now. His voice sounded steeped, moist. "Nowhere."

The girl nodded and asked one more thing—"Hungry?" Before he could reply, assuming his answer, she turned to go. She was way ahead of him—not actually, they went side by side.

"I'm Shane," she said.

"Ranger," he said, and both their names were like places or positions or inanimate objects, something else they had in common.

Then he saw where she lived.

It was a real house—with a front door and working windows on its several floors. It had even been painted sometime in the last century or some other time Ranger couldn't understand. It was completely isolated on its block, where only suggestions of once towering, now obliterated structures were scattered on either end.

"Come on," Shane said and took his hand, a touch which while innocent (and he had removed his gloves), at fifteen sent a shiver through him.

The two went through the front door, and it was immediately cool inside, though he heard no hum of air conditioner or fan. The house was sparsely furnished, with worn pieces that appeared to have been picked off the street, some even charred or hobbled from their own explosions. Ranger smelled a weird and dizzying mix of baked bread and—was it steak or chicken? He had had so little meat in his life that he couldn't tell.

"You're just in time for dinner."

It was a woman's voice. Emerging from around a corner was in fact a woman, probably as old as Brenda but looking older because she was unadorned. Her hair had gone gray (Brenda kept hers the color of fire) and she was soft and billowing where Brenda was hemmed-in and taut. Maybe it was her sort of sack dress, which moved here and there, relaxed and playfully indifferent, as she came forward, unlike the military stiffness of Brenda's shirt and skirt. In her oven-mitted hands was the bread Ranger had thought was there, smoking benignly and in a basket.

"I brought a guest," Shane said.

The woman stopped and looked at Ranger. For a second, her face registered confusion; this was quickly replaced by an expression he took to be welcoming but had seen rarely and not recently at all.

"Okay," she said. "I'm Marilyn. Shane's mother."

Ranger didn't answer, surprised. He thought Shane's not saying her own last name meant that she was orphaned. Now he knew it was her just being easy, friendly, and informal.

These qualities were present in the way they ate, too: sitting at a big table in a dining room with open windows on every side. Somewhere else, Ranger might have felt on display, imprisoned, and judged. Here he sensed they were hiding nothing, were celebrating themselves, and offering up places for still others to take.

"This is delicious," he said, chewing—steak, it turned out—deliberately, to appreciate each bite. The conversation was casual and considerate—no one asked him prying questions; it was as if he were a soldier and they didn't wish to remind him of the carnage he had witnessed or caused. Still, they didn't avoid the issue altogether.

"It's so sad about the club," Marilyn said.

"It seemed hopeful that they'd built it on that block," Shane added.

"Like the neighborhood was coming back."

"Right. But no."

"It turned out to be just another target."

Shane and Marilyn had a rapport that fascinated Ranger. They didn't quite finish each other's sentences, but their words were connected, as if holding hands; he was embarrassed to imagine such a corny thing, but they'd inspired it. What most impressed Ranger about the meal (besides the food, of course—and that included the homemade dessert of some kind of fruit pie; he wasn't familiar enough with fruit to know which one it was) was Marilyn's focus on him. When she wasn't overtly observing him, she was sneaking peeks at him from across the table. Ranger had always been studied with suspicion by others to, say, see he didn't steal (which he sometimes did, of course). But this woman watched him with worry; her glance was the equivalent of someone kissing his forehead for a fever, something no one had ever done. He could not help leaning in to catch more of her concern, as if it were the spray of the sprinkler that had cooled down orphan kids when he was little (sometimes increasing until it was strong enough to wash them all away; it had been a trick to flick them off a street). Marilyn meant for him to be bathed in it, he could tell; this time he wasn't making it up or misinterpreting, as he did so often other people's intentions, unused as he was to and craving as he did human kindness. When she cleared the dishes and left the room, declining his help, acting as if he had exerted himself enough today, it was as if the room grew dark and dull without her.

"You're staying over, right?" Shane asked, but it wasn't a question, a double-check.

Later, Ranger lay on a big bare mattress in an otherwise empty room on the ground floor. He curled up there like a baby too young to have a blanket, not strong enough to keep from suffocating beneath it. Shane brought him a thin sheet, decorated with lambs and a female shepherd he didn't know was named Bo Peep. She draped it over him solemnly, the way you would a human sacrifice, which made them both laugh.

"I don't usually use one," she said, "but you might get cold."

Lying face down, already almost asleep, he felt the mattress shake. And Ranger understood: this was where Shane slept, too.

The bed was big enough that he barely knew she was near him, and she didn't pull on or ask to share the sheet. Still, with the filmy fabric over his ears, he could hear her breathe. He glanced down at the foot of the mattress and saw her shoes, shorts and shirt piled on the floor, a pair of white underpants on top, like the scoop of vanilla ice cream that had been on the pie for dessert. He had removed his own clothes already.

Ranger curled into a smaller ball, bent on creating more distance between them. Yet he couldn't keep from getting hard, his penis like a rock between his thighs with which he couldn't help but hit someone. This shifted the sheet, exposing a shoulder, and Shane lifted and placed it back on him, as a sister might. It fluttered there like a tongue and, helplessly, he ejaculated, careful to catch the cum with his thighs so as not to stain the sheet before he passed out again. The next thing he knew he was on his back, his legs completely spread, the sheet kicked to his feet, hot wet sunlight pouring on him like concrete, and Shane was gone.

Ranger moved into the house. Whatever stuff he had in the church didn't matter—he kept most of what he needed on his person, and the Beamer had been lost. He did chores around the place; even the nearly empty areas needed cleaning. Sometimes he was given money by Marilyn for food and ventured out to the few stores open in the neighborhood; other times, he negotiated with people on the street who hoarded goods. There were neighborhoods like Brenda's that had good security and so had not been devastated, and he would secretly travel there to bring back better things. Whenever he returned, Marilyn gave him that worried look he loved.

At night, they would gather around Shane's small device and squint to watch films or TV shows. Neither woman asked him anything about his life; they still treated this time as his convalescence. In fact, Ranger was so exhausted he slept long hours, often with Shane beside him, on the bed bare but for the sheet. He did not consciously touch her, but sometimes he would wake up wet again and wonder what had happened. One morning, he found a pubic hair (not his own) in his mouth, and Shane again was gone. They didn't say anything about it but blushed when they were alone, doing the dishes or something.

Ranger noticed that he looked older now. He soon found shaving equipment and a deodorant left for him on the glass ledge beneath the bathroom mirror. He taught himself how to use the razor and cut his nose, lip, chin, and cheek, which made the woman both sympathize with and laugh a little at him.

Occasionally, in one of his shallower sleeps, he would hear what he believed were bomb blasts from blocks away, reduced to dull thuds in the distance. If he remembered in the morning, he would check news sources and read about another event or upscale venue successfully targeted. Ranger would bitterly wonder who Brenda had sent out to scour it—Trey? Was that that little weasel's name? Then he forced himself to forget.

Sometimes, he would open the door to strangers seeking Marilyn who had no interest in talking or even leaving a message with anyone else. One of these people smelled of sulfur and another was out of breath. There were calls, too, and texts for her that Ranger answered or by accident intercepted.

"I forgot to mention," he began to say, one night in bed. Then he told Shane about such a visitor. Lying beside him, Shane didn't answer for a second, and Ranger almost fell asleep before she did.

"Did they say anything?"

"Who? Oh. No."

"You take a message?"

"Sorry. Should I have?"

"No. It's fine. Forget it." And her last two words didn't seem a suggestion but something stricter. This was another time that Ranger woke up feeling he'd experienced an exciting event while asleep—his skin was tingling—and wasn't sure if it had been a dream.

Then Marilyn apparently decided she had left Ranger alone long enough. At their next dinner, she asked him questions. They felt to Ranger like she was opening his Army backpack, trying to get a sense of what was inside, the way a mother would want to know how far in deed and feeling her soldier son had gone from her.

"You used to work for someone?" she asked, passing delicious mashed potatoes to soften him up.

Ranger nodded, giving himself a scoop of the creamy, highly buttered stuff.

"Not for yourself?"

"No. How could I do that?" It was the first "attitude" he had shown since coming, a sign that he was either more at ease or suddenly threatened. Either way, it surprised him to hear.

"Who was it? Brenda?"

Ranger had just slapped potato on the piece of steak he was about to stick in his mouth, so it looked like a white toupee on top. Now it slid a little down the side as the question made him stop. "Yeah." He popped it into his mouth, making it impossible for him to say more. How'd she know about Brenda?

"Right," she said, as if it was obvious. "Did she fire you?"

"No. I quit." *Are you kidding me?* he wanted to say, but kept his head.

Marilyn nodded, as if having figured that much, he was glad to see. Her tone changed as she herself stopped eating and watched him. "You tell her why?"

"No."

"Just walked away?"

"Yes." He didn't mention Trey; that might make him seem small.

"Have you been in touch with her since you left?"

Ranger looked up, pressing a piece of bread into gravy as a child would his boot into a puddle. The inquiries were starting to annoy him. "Of course not. You've been here. You've seen me."

"Maybe you should let her know you're okay."

Ranger didn't reply. Marilyn's tone was the aural equivalent of her worried looks; there was a warmth to it that he was unfamiliar with. Yet he didn't delight in it as he did her glances, which he still sought out. The questions made him realize her attention could be rigorous, her love (and he knew that's what it was, he wasn't stupid) required things of him; it didn't allow him everything. He didn't like that.

When you were neglected—dismissed, even loathed—you were left alone.

"Why don't you go see her?" she said.

Ranger wanted to tell her to stop, stop pressing me, let me eat in peace, just—look at me, that's all I want. Instead, surprising himself even more, he blurted out, "Because she's finished with me, that's why."

He was quiet after this and done with his dinner, pushing away his plate. He knew this contradicted what he'd said before, that he'd quit. But he didn't mean it literally: Brenda had let him go, not fired him, there was a difference. And now he spat out a sudden cry that was like rotten wet meat choking him, covered his face with his hands, sticky from the buttered bread, and wept.

Marilyn let him; she didn't interrupt. When he could cry no more, he realized his moans had silenced all other sounds. His ears cleared, the way they do when you descend from a great height. He heard Marilyn sigh, with compassion.

"I'm sure," she said, "that that's not true."

Marilyn made and packed him a lunch, which she amusedly said she wanted to wrap in a napkin and put on a stick at his shoulder; but he'd never read Tom Sawyer or any similar story, so he didn't reply. She wrote a note, told him, "This is for Brenda, not you," folded it twice and placed it in his back pocket, where the Beamer once had been. He would have to find his way there and back on his own.

"Can you do that?" she asked.

"Yes," he said, without thinking.

Ranger looked for Shane to say goodbye, but she wasn't around, and she'd already been asleep when he'd come to bed. He had a funny feeling she was avoiding him, he didn't know why. He remembered that he had been recently interpreting things negatively, so he stopped. Still, it felt as if Shane had done her job, the way a worm is finished when a fish hangs on its hook. Ranger hated the image, but he had it in his head, he couldn't help it.

He retraced his steps to Brenda's. This time, there was more life the longer he went in reverse: buildings were reconstructed, people existed again. When Ranger entered her office, he expected to see a crowd of new kids there—conscripts, he now considered them; this was how Marilyn and Shane had made him feel. But the waiting area was empty and, though Brenda's door was open, he heard nothing from within. Ranger advanced and stepped onto its threshold as if approaching a precipice.

Brenda was behind her desk, staring right at him. Her new device—was it one even newer?—lay discarded on the reflecting surface of her black desk, as if having revealed something she'd rejected. Suddenly, he couldn't remember how long he'd been gone. A month? Six? Brenda appeared older, but maybe it was he who had aged. She looked at him as if he'd been a child when he left and was no longer.

"Look who's here," she said.

Ranger didn't know how to reply: her tone was as closed-off and hard-boiled as ever and allowed him no way in. And her look, unlike Marilyn's, didn't land on him like a soothing hand but went through him without stopping and hit the wall at his back.

He waited, wondering if she might communicate with him as she always had, by sparring and giving him a job. But she only blinked, expecting him to say the next word or make the first move. The situation was both the same as when he'd left and worse, for he'd hoped it would be different.

He threw the note on Brenda's desk.

"What's that?" she said.

It was weird: each woman communicated in this archaic way, which was both personal and perishable, a form that highlighted one's handwriting with all its looping and stabbing idiosyncrasies that could be removed and never recovered, unlike a computer file or a person whose DNA he scooped up. It was as if both Brenda and Marilyn knew their relationship with him was temporal and would exist longer in his memory than in any other way.

"See for yourself," he said.

She looked at him as if he knew what it contained. Yet Ranger had obeyed Marilyn and had not read it.

Brenda unfolded the paper and didn't blink for the short time it took her to take it in. Then she closed and placed her hand upon it, not letting Ranger have it, keeping it between the two of them, Marilyn and her.

Ranger had assumed the note was an explanation—even an apology—for why she'd kept Ranger so long, where he'd been, what he'd done. Yet it was too short to have said all that. And Brenda's expression had if anything hardened; if she understood anything better now, the knowledge hadn't made her more compassionate.

"Thanks," was all she said.

Ranger waited and kept waiting, but she wouldn't be the one to break the silence or crack a smile. He knew he was stronger than when he'd left and swore he would not be the one to weaken first. Yet Ranger also knew that Brenda was still better at this than he. Helplessly, he exhaled and in the breath came his capitulation, a question released like a dead rat flushed from a drainpipe.

"You got anything for me?"

There was silence again. Ranger's heart sped up. A smirk came onto Brenda's mouth, lifting the right side of her upper lip, plumping her cheek, and closing one eye: everything connected, nothing accidental; dismissing him was an instinct. Then she stopped as if it were petty—unprofessional—to take pleasure in his defeat.

"No," she said. "Sorry." And she reached for her device— to, what, call another kid?

Ranger left, his face burning, lacerated by losing to her once more when he'd been most determined to win. He rode the Trus and Brain back to Marilyn's, the journey more than memorized, now second nature. He was never going back to Brenda, that bitch, whom he hated now; he had not been able to even think the word before.

As he went, the landscape was again stripped of features; there was less and less to look at. He saw the bones of buildings, only parts of people, and felt this was his future, where he belonged. Goodbye to Brenda, that bitch, whom he hated. He had a real home now and was almost there.

When he got on the street again, rain fell, as hard as he had ever seen it, hurting when it hit his face, like a door opening on him again and again. Ranger hadn't brought an umbrella; that was for weaklings and anyway would have done nothing in a deluge. The water soaked then melted away his shirt; he peeled it off in pieces and made his way to Marilyn's in shorts, looking at last like someone's diapered child.

Yet he couldn't get inside. A pair of policemen stood guard, preventing anyone from approaching.

"What's going on?" he asked.

One cop looked at him with the usual contempt and didn't answer.

"I got to get in," Ranger said.

"Why? There's not a lot to steal." Snide, hurtful.

"Because I live there now, that's why."

Now the cop didn't find him funny. "Go away."

While Ranger was technically retired, it did not mean he had lost his skills. He quickly employed a move that was part limbo dance, part sliding into home, though he had never heard of either thing. Before the cop realized it, he was inside.

In the few minutes he was free, Ranger saw no evidence of anyone living there; and in the skewed position of his mattress, the broken cups in the kitchen, and—unless he was hallucinating—the small bloodstains on the wall, signs of a struggle that had ended badly. There was a faint aroma of baking bread, but he thought it might have been his imagination.

This time, the police were not jaded about his escape but made to apprehend him.

"Where are they?" Ranger asked, as they held his arms so he wouldn't hit them anymore.

Ranger slept in the hall, for the door was locked. He had escaped the police and didn't want to lose any time before finding the person he thought responsible.

Waking him, Brenda's door opened.

Had she slept there, as he had? Did she always stay in the office, have no other home? Was there even more they had in common? Brenda looked down at him as if at the delivery of something she had not ordered. Then, saying nothing, she turned and went back in.

Ranger stumbled after her, sick with fatigue. Never facing or addressing him, the older woman opened her blinds and let in the rude morning light. For a second, he understood and marveled at the fact that she worked there alone, except for freelancers. She was the only permanent person. When everything was exposed, Brenda moved toward her desk.

"What," Ranger said, "were you jealous?"

"Me? Of who?" She took no time to consider the question.

"Did you make up some story? Tell the cops a stupid lie about her?" Before she could answer, Ranger started screaming: how much he had always hated her, how he hated her so much now, he would kill her if he could. Because Brenda wouldn't have him but wouldn't let anyone else. He had no control over what he said. Ranger couldn't stop and soon was unable to express any words. He was in pieces, his heart on a spike like those remains at the club.

When Brenda hit him, it wasn't to stop him, to slap sense into him, like an actor in an old movie he hadn't seen. Brenda didn't seem motivated by helping him with tough love or whatever the ancient expression was. She seemed spurred on by anger alone, by the need to shut him up.

After she had finished yelling—calling him every name for "fool," whacking him back and forth with both hands, as Ranger covered his face and sank to his knees, not fighting back—she picked up the piece of paper given to him by Marilyn. She dropped it on him as if it were a final, crushing stone. It fluttered from his face to his feet.

"Read it," she said, panting, "for God's sake."

At first, Ranger didn't move, shaken as much by his own reaction to Brenda as Brenda's to him. Sniffing back a drowning wave of salty water, his fingers trembling, he reached for the note, opened it, and did as he was told.

Ranger was just a good enough reader to get the gist. It was an offer from one woman to the other. Marilyn said that she knew when bombings occurred because they were done by her people. If she shared this information with Brenda, her freelancers could arrive on the scene before anyone else and give the Muth Co. first dibs on the remains. An arrangement could be worked out between them and relayed by Ranger, who could be their carrier pigeon. There was no mention of alerting the authorities and stopping the bombings before they took place.

Ranger dropped the paper on the floor, where it lay open. He imagined fumes flying from it, smoke the result of pestilence, the steam off shit. He looked up at Brenda and felt it was fitting that she loomed above him. She was better than Marilyn, whom she had punished. In the world in which he lived, Brenda was good. She had tried to protect him. It was the most and only love he would ever get.

"Now go to sleep." Brenda nodded at the couch in the corner, before leaving the room. "You don't want to fuck up your next job."

Ranger lay down on the lumpy couch. He slowly became unconscious, curled like an infant, with stubble on his face. Ranger would be sixteen in a month. He would never leave Brenda again, and she would never again hire any other boy.

The New Year's Resolution

The city was so quiet, it seemed uninhabited. It had been this way ever since the wealthy became the only ones who could afford to live there, the wealthy from other countries who deigned to drop in on their way to their apartments in London or Moscow or Beijing (the homeless being the only ones who shared the city with them).

New Year's Day was especially quiet, Abigail thought; even the rich who *had* alighted on the city were gone. No one was stumbling home after a drunken one-night stand; there was no discharged vomit on the street, no discarded cone hats. No one was even sleeping it off; Abigail herself had been up for hours, and it was only eight o'clock. She was flying out that day, had chosen this return date because there'd be the fewest passengers on the plane.

Abigail always lived like this, avoiding people. She had flown in to see her parents in the suburbs for Christmas yet insisted on staying alone in town at the apartment of a (rich, foreign) friend abandoned until January 2nd. She would be returning to the smaller city where she lived and worked at home, online, rarely seeing her employers. She felt accosted by people, accused by them, unprepared for what they would expect of her, which she would only fail to provide. To her, any human encounter was like a mugging if she was without a purse; she feared she would be killed for what she did not carry.

Being alone had become an obligation. She owed it to herself, though made miserable and exhausted by it: crying at night, curled on her bed, masturbating, frantically, rubbing at herself as if trying to remove the tag on a mattress she'd been told to leave alone. Abigail felt like a junkie who could no longer find a vein, longing to quit because there was no way to continue.

"Oh, no," said Rory, the man in her bed.

This day—this year—would be different. Resolutions were the corniest kind of cliché, but who cared? She had made one. She'd started by leaving her parents' New Year's Eve party early (and what party? The two of them sitting before the TV, watching the huge celebration held in a midtown square, now attended only by computer-generated crowds and green-screened minor celebrities since there were no longer enough residents or tourists? Was it *their* reclusiveness that Abigail had inherited? Probably). Then she'd gone to a bar after arriving at the train station.

It was one of the few crowded places in town, one of many in the chain called "Dive," made to replicate the sleazy environs of earlier times. Obscene graffiti had been pre-placed on walls treated to look filthy, wooden bar tops came complete with knife marks made by children in factories far away, and a urine smell had been added to pristine commodes. The customers were not down-at-the-heel drinkers but other sons and daughters of the suburbs who had caught trains tonight to drink in a simulacrum of somewhere sinful.

Rory was one of the few actually from the city itself, he said—screamed—as others sang and laughed deafeningly around them.

"My mom and dad were in the same apartment forever," he said. "They moved in when it was affordable. My dad is dead and my mom and I live there now."

Abigail didn't ask his age but thought he was a little younger than she, in his mid-twenties, and even more lanky—lithe was the word. (They had carded Rory when he ordered a drink, and she hadn't been surprised.) She concentrated on his appealing face so as not to dwell on the pushing, clawing people who had penned them in, so close she felt they were like planks in a floorboard but standing up, if that made any sense; she would have been hysterical if not for him.

Abigail never drank, not needing another reason to be at a distance, and Rory nursed the one he was holding before he asked, "Would you want to go outside?"

She believed he had picked up on her discomfort and good sport effort to fit in, and that this meant that he was sensitive.

"Yes," Abigail said. "Thanks."

The two forced their way out, elbowing, rolling, and ramming, and she was reminded of the drills that burrowed through and displaced the dirt when they had first built the subways, that's how hard it was to do.

"Jeez," she said when they made it to the deserted block. "I thought I'd die in there."

Abigail had said it facetiously; this was as much as she'd reveal of her anxiety; why unnerve him when they'd just met? Still, how could he *not* notice the sweat on her face and neck, at her underarms, and the small of her back, which had soaked through her blouse? And it wasn't even as warm as it usually was on New Year's Eve; it was only seventy.

Yet Rory hadn't noticed. He had his own preoccupation. He was looking for the best place to bend slightly and throw up, which is what he proceeded to do, aiming at the side of the "Dive" door, barely missing the top step of a laundry nearby, which had its front door one floor down.

Afterwards, Rory shook his head, dismayed by the damage he'd done, his face illuminated and revealed to be pale by the bar's blinking syringe logo. Abigail realized he had not asked her outside to help but because he'd been about to be ill.

"How many did you have before I got there?" she asked.

"That was my first," he said, and she decided he may not have been sensitive but at least he had a sense of humor.

"How far do you live from here?" she asked, wondering if he could get home all right.

"Three stops," he said, his voice raw.

"My place is closer. I mean, my friend's place." She felt this information had been organically offered. She hadn't pushed or pulled or created it artificially, the way a magician did a bouquet from his cane, and she was impressed with herself.

Rory didn't take the hint, just swallowed with difficulty and seemed to sway a bit. So, Abigail completely rebelled against her internal resistance and saw the drills start spinning again underground until they broke through and brought huge amounts of light and dust down on her. "Would you like to come over?"

In the apartment, Rory was quiet and polite, like a child on his best behavior, which was bad (she wished them to misbehave, in the old-fashioned sense of the word) and good (she felt young, too, or at least inexperienced). He sat in a chair with his hands in his lap, balanced there as he might two teacups filled to the brim. He became more attractive the longer Abigail looked at him, less young, with appealing little wrinkles around each eye, though they might have been temporary, made by the stress of nausea or something; that didn't make much sense, either, but she was nervous.

Since Rory was not initiating anything, Abigail knelt on the floor before him, placed her hands on his knees, spread his legs apart unintentionally, which was awkward, like she was doing the Charleston, that old dance, *for* him, and kissed his lips, pressing in her tongue, tasting just the mouthwash strips he'd swallowed on the walk there, nothing nasty, well, maybe just a memory of the (how many?) vodkas he had, a combination which was young and old, like him, and aroused her. Then she pulled back, having gotten little participation, though she sensed he found it pleasurable. Rory soon explained.

"I'm sorry," he said, but he was still too sick for sex. He wasn't more apologetic and didn't appear embarrassed, which was a relief; either would have made him seem insecure or insincere. "Can we just sleep?"

Abigail was touched by his directness and physical misery. At least he wasn't leaving; that would have meant her resolution was kaput right away and cut into her confidence.

"Okay," she said.

Rory slept soundly, utterly at ease in someone else's bed, unlike Abigail, who was unhinged by his presence and restless, she couldn't help it.

In the morning, Abigail awoke surprised she'd slept at all. She saw that he was already up, sitting beside her, his back against the wall, going through his messages. Shirtless, Rory looked even scrawnier, still sickly, and completely caught up in what he was seeing or not seeing, she wasn't sure, on his phone.

Abigail stood and checked out the window, hoping he'd notice that she was nude (he was still also in his underwear) which he didn't—or maybe he didn't want her to *know* he'd noticed, maybe that was it. Maybe there was still hope, she thought. Anyway, this was when she perceived that the city was silent and right before she heard him say, in an obviously upset response to what had just appeared or not appeared on his device:

"Oh, no."

"What is it?" she asked, because he seemed to be requesting her attention (or had she just imagined it?).

For a second, Rory hesitated, as if the thing was too private to share. Then he came to a conclusion. "It's nothing."

Still, he kept sighing, staring at the same spot on his phone, maybe testing her, seeing if she'd keep advancing, as it were, the more he pushed her away.

Abigail did. She reached over and placed her hand softly on his device (it was a new one, the small square that opened like an accordion but showed no sign of the screen having been folded; she didn't understand the science). He let it slip from his fingers and she cradled it, bringing it close enough to her face—she wasn't wearing her glasses—that her breath fogged the screen. She felt more intimate with him at that moment than in all the time they'd been in bed.

Abigail read a message from the police. They informed Rory that an intoxicated woman named Naomi had fallen down on a midtown street. She'd been identified by a neighbor and taken to a nearby hospital, where she was being held for observation in Intensive Care. If he was interested, he could call this number or go to the hospital itself, thank you, and Happy New Year.

"She always picks the holidays to do this," Rory said. "That's when she gets the most attention. Or maybe when she's the loneliest, I don't know. My mother, I mean."

He had added the identification as if he'd forgotten he hadn't clarified this and didn't want to assume she knew. He was aware of Abigail now, in other words, which she appreciated. Their fingers touched together briefly as she passed back the phone, which she now knew was an important piece of him, a connecting cord to someone else. His skin was hot.

"She's been drunk, basically, ever since my father died five years ago," Rory confessed to her, switching to dependence from seeming obliviousness, "and usually ends up in the hospital."

Abigail nodded, saying nothing, waiting for him to go on. His breathing had grown as fast as hers had been when she emerged from the bar.

"I better go," he said.

Rory flew from the bed, the way cartoon characters bolt and leave puffs of smoke behind. The phone fell into the sheets, forgotten. He turned to retrieve it, not knowing for an instant which way to go—that is, he was desperate to go forward but confused how to handle what he left behind. She helped him, picked up and offered the phone to him in cupped hands, as if it now was water from a well that would restore him. He took it with great and obvious gratitude. How could he not ask what she secretly wished him to?

"Want to come with me?"

Rory's mother was being kept behind a curtain in the Emergency Room. As the only hospital left in the city, the place was inundated by the homeless. Abigail was impressed that, of all those suffering there, it was his mother the physicians felt should be shielded. Was it for her protection or other people's?

"Please wait here," Rory said as if protecting *her*, too. Before she could insist on accompanying him, he was out of earshot, approaching the exhausted female nurse who slumped like a wounded sentry at the curtain's opening. As he was allowed in, Abigail saw a flash of a bruised, bloated, and elderly female face before the cloth, decorated by crowns, covered it again.

Behind the curtain, Abigail heard a high-pitched cry and the slurred words, "So glad to see you!" Then there was a lower-pitched demurral and impatient whispers as what sounded like a squabble began. The higher voice grew more insistent and piercing until it rang through the waiting room, like a broken bell warning of disaster in the year ahead. Now Abigail knew what they had hoped the curtain might mask.

Suddenly, Rory came back out. He—who had recently seemed to age—looked even younger and more vulnerable, an overwrought child announcing the cancellation of his little play, closing the curtain to cover the "disaster."

"Let's go," he said, reaching Abigail. He muttered something unintelligible, which meant there's no talking to her, she's impossible, I can't take it anymore.

"Do you want *me* to try?" Abigail said—blurted out, really. Rory just squinted in response, as if at a bright light, saying nothing. So, Abigail marched toward the curtain, heeding only her need to become more involved with humanity this New Year's Day.

As she approached, the sounds of piping distress grew marked from the obscured area. Abigail opened the curtain, startling the nurse who was attending to Rory's mother, adjusting an IV in the back of the old woman's hand, flesh falling and falling from her bones like tears.

"Who are you?" Naomi yelled, loud enough to shoot through the emergency room again.

Panicked, Abigail fiddled closed the curtain behind her, as if it were her own hospital gown. "I'm a friend of Rory's." Abigail expected the nurse to shoo her out, but the pooped attendant seemed thrilled to be spelled and, once the drip was secured, left the two of them alone. "Abigail."

"Are you his girlfriend?" Naomi rummaged through her flooded mind and grabbed what she could of her maternal wariness.

"No," Abigail said, but Naomi didn't get it; the answer was too complicated.

"That's nice," she said. "I bet you're worried. Are you worried?"

"About what?"

The old woman leaned forward, offering a comical confidence. "I've heard his mother's a lush."

Abigail smiled, surprised by the other's whimsicality, though she could tell Naomi believed herself a mere tippler, not the addict she actually was.

"Is that right?" Abigail tried to think of something clever. "That's too bad. But I bet she's very nice."

Naomi shrugged, tired of the banter. On her collapsed face, Abigail could see the remains of beauty, the way one spies a painting beneath another in a frame, through rips in the one on top. Naomi started to rush, trying to outrun the sobriety which would soon overtake and send her into withdrawal, the screams but a preview of what was to come. Or did she sense her days on Earth were severely limited? How many more times could she fall down, after all? The black-purple swelling adorned her left temple like a wrestler's tattoo.

"Look," she said, sharing another secret, this one in earnest, "it runs in my family. But he doesn't have to worry."

"Who? About what?"

"Rory. We had him altered."

Abigail said nothing, not catching on. Naomi proceeded to explain, reciting information that she had obviously long ago memorized.

In vitro, she said, Rory had had gene therapy to encode proteins that converted alcohol into acetaldehyde and then acetate, making drinking toxic for him. It mimicked the natural mutation common in, say, Asian people, that could make them sickened even by the tiny amount of alcohol found in mouthwash.

"*You* know what I mean." Rory's mother pointed a fluttery finger. Even though Abigail was Korean American, she'd never had a physical aversion to booze, just an emotional one. But she did not reply.

"He was never told," Naomi said, softly, her energy even for going crazy running out. "We thought it best that way. We worried he'd think he was a puppet. When it was really just the opposite. He's so sensitive, there's no talking to him sometimes." Did she mean herself? Or both herself and her son? In any case, she had given him a gift.

Naomi laid her mottled and translucent hand upon Abigail's. "Please take care of him, honey."

The hand slipped from hers, and Naomi fell back on her pillow as if from a great height. In a second, she was snoring softly. The effort had been too much for her, yet she'd thought it important to try. Rory's mother had kept her own resolution, Abigail thought, using in another way the day she often exploited for attention.

Abigail exited and saw Rory against a wall. He was staring at his phone again, this time for diversion, his face blank, as if each new thing he saw administered more of a sedating agent. He had just enough energy to lift his head and ask, with trepidation,

"How is she?"

Abigail shrugged and didn't answer. She walked out of the emergency room and then the hospital itself. Rory followed, growing more eager for illumination as the entrancing effect of all that information wore off.

"Is she—"

"She's fine." Abigail stopped near the cul de sac that brought in the ambulances. "Look, why don't you come home with me?"

"Now?"

"Yes. Not here. Back where I really live. There'll be room on the plane. There always is. Most everyone greets the New Year unconscious. We're already not doing that. You don't have to stay for long. I'd like your company."

Abigail was surprised by how easy this had been to express. She had been infused by Naomi's determination, inherited her will right before it had been destroyed, with the old woman's complicity stealing her commitment at the very last second.

Yet she saw that Rory was not okay with it. He blinked a few times, unnerved. Then he shook his head at what was unimaginable. "But who will take care of my mom?"

Abigail looked at him, a portrait of childish helplessness, his sparse and unattended stubble the only evidence of his being an adult. She knew there was a way to make him mature and free. The old woman had wanted it. Still, Abigail was aware she was also doing it for herself.

So, she told Rory how he had been engineered, as best as she could, given her limited comprehension of genetic existence. She haltingly repeated what his mother had revealed, leaving out only the Asian part (she considered including it as a way to make them similar—since that was what Naomi had tried to do—but gave up).

"That's why you were so sick after just one drink," she ended with, understanding that he'd told the truth.

After she was quiet, Rory did not respond. His face held an expression of incredulity and both things made Abigail panic. Did he think it had been ridiculous to listen to his mother? Of course he did. In her condition, even at her best, she would have been raving.

Abigail felt like a fool for spreading the lie; she'd been desperate, and, like most desperate people, she'd pushed away what she'd wished to attain.

Then, suddenly, studying him, Abigail knew she was wrong. Rory felt she was naive about something *else*. He pushed out a big, scoffing breath.

"I *know* that," he said. "Don't you think I *know* that?"

Rory said nothing more. He turned and stared at a storefront across the street. It was a faux-Irish pub that had opened for lunch, one of the few bars in the neighborhood doing business today. Rory crossed against the light since there were no cars. He disappeared through its small, dark, and aromatic opening, where he would stay forever. He didn't ask if Abigail would come.

Abigail stood unmoving for a minute. Dreading to admit failure, she was about to follow. Then she realized she was perilously close to missing her plane. She started back toward her friend's apartment.

As she walked, she became aware of the homeless on the street, the city's only remaining natives, also attached to what didn't sustain them. Abigail opened up and emptied her wallet, handing off every bill she had to them. She did the same with her coins. Was it a fee to belong, the kind she'd pay to start a lease in the New Year? Or was it a ransom, a way to escape? Abigail made a decision.

She would stay the night and take a flight tomorrow, one that would be filled with more people. It would cost her, she thought; there'd be a price for changing. Abigail knew there always was.

The Image of His Parents

Guy was very special to his parents, very dear, as they used to say. By the time he entered his late childhood, he had been subject to more supervision, worry, and love than most kids ever were. In the view of these other kids and some adult observers (such as myself), this had given him the demeanor of a little prince. During his first check-up after he turned ten, I noticed that he was perfect, and perhaps this was a problem.

"There's nothing wrong with you at all," I said.

"That's good, right?" Guy asked. He was young enough not to know what I meant but old enough to know that I meant *something*.

"No scraped knees, no scars, no broken nose. That kind of wrong."

I let this sink in, willing to accept that it wouldn't and that we would merely move on. Still, I gave the boy enough time to pursue the topic if he pleased.

"Sure," he said, "I've never done anything where that might happen. I haven't been allowed by my mom and dad."

"Exactly."

"And that's a good thing. Right?"

Guy wanted me to attach a value to his perfection, if you will. His parents—my old friends, Ruthie and Magnus—answered *everything* for him, disallowed his making his own interpretations and possibly making a mistake or suffering an upset. This was what he expected all adults to do. Since I'd known the boy since birth, you could have called me his slightly disreputable uncle, though fun uncle would have been my preference. In any case, my relationship with him went beyond family doctor, so I wanted to do something different. Yet I didn't push my privilege and proceeded cautiously.

"I don't know," I said. "What do *you* think?"

When Guy grew silent, I saw aspects of both his parents in him: Ruthie's emotional engagement with life and Magnus's need for control. He seemed more plagued than intrigued by the problem I'd created, and I'd wanted to inspire, not disturb him. Even though I knew this was exactly what his parents always did, I gave in.

"It's not a bad thing," I said. He visibly brightened at my categorizing his condition, my letting him off the hook, which revealed to me my lack of guts. I wanted to maintain some self-respect and at least help him a *little* bit. "But sometimes you learn things by being…"

"Hurt?" This scared him.

"No." I hoped he would want, not fear, what I wanted for him. "Free."

"Oh."

The word clearly struck a nerve, just as I had lightly struck his knee with a little hammer. After a second, Guy nodded. I left him alone in the exam room and retired to my den-like office where I awaited his appearance, giving him time to process what I'd said.

When at last he appeared, Guy did in fact look different. Older? Or was it my self-aggrandizing imagination that I could have had that kind of impact?

"So, what do I do?" he asked.

I played dumb. "Just keep doing what you're doing. You're in good health."

"No." This would have been hard for an actual adult to ask, let alone a boy. "What do I do to be free?"

"Oh." I shrugged, partly because I didn't know and partly because I didn't want to be responsible in case something terrible happened.

"That's up to you," I said.

Guy nodded again, disappointed: adults had always been prescriptive and unequivocal about right and wrong. Yet I saw—or at least imagined—excitement start to color his face as the first evidence of acne was doing.

"Okay," he said and accepted the challenge.

I was about to say, "Good," but decided that even that word was too opinionated. I simply wrote him a prescription for pimple cream, as if it were my blessing.

Guy left my office and went outside. Through my window, I saw that he looked around, as if expecting someone. In the near distance, a self-driving car approached. I assumed it had been pre-arranged by his parents, for Guy's phone could only receive calls not make them.

The boy saw the vehicle and began to raise his hand as a signal. Then he suddenly darted the other way and disappeared behind a bush to the right of my window. He stayed there, stock still, panting, just beyond my eye line. We were side by side, unseen by the other, watching, as the car stopped and huffed as if impatient. At last, with what seemed reluctance, it drove away without him.

Guy stepped out from his hiding place. Through the glass, I saw him proudly brush brambles from his shoulders, as if they were epaulets marking his promotion.

I knew he was thinking: Where to now?

Guy's phone could not be turned off, either—it was controlled by his parents at the other end. Still, he did the best he could to disable it, placing it on the bottom of his backpack, where the sound would be muffled by his books (the volume, too, was not his to raise or lower). Then he took off on foot in the opposite direction from his home.

After a mile or two, Guy stopped, out of breath, on the scuff-resistant asphalt of our suburb's streets. Before him was the entrance to Mossy Trails, the huge, man-made park that had replaced one of our abandoned malls.

Guy walked through the entrance, a raised wreath-like configuration made of recycled plastic and filtered human waste. He knew that cameras captured his image at each step as they did everyone's in town, courtesy of his father, who had made and installed them. Yet he didn't care or was willing to take the risk since I had put the bug of rebellion in his ear (along with my otoscope, of course).

Guy raced past a massive and immaculate lawn, its turf composed of ground-up coconut fertilized by cornmeal and seaweed, the wafting aromas of fish, salad, and dessert: the smell of freedom. On his left was a small lake, the water of which was rippled glass, surrounded by animatronic children whose little sail boats moved by remote control. Before him were the woods, where trees were concoctions of treated silk, their imperfections and poisons removed. This was where Guy ran.

None of it had been rational. He had acted like an animal escaping out a back door, a pet tied up for years against its will, more disobedient than Ginger, the loyal and now dead dog of his infancy whom he didn't recall. Guy was more animal than the creatures surrounding him, the puppet deer, chipmunks, birds, beetles, and worms that had been modeled on cartoons.

Soon he sensed a human behind him.

Guy didn't know what made him aware of it. He'd heard and seen nothing: no expelled sigh, no leaves or twigs cracking (not that the grain-made ground would make a noise). He had simply picked up on an aura. Guy turned slowly, afraid.

In the near distance was a figure. It was decked out in androgynous drag: plaid shirt, cargo pants, and a cap pulled low enough to obscure the face, as if in parody of a rich landowner surveying an estate. The only thing missing was a trusty hound retrieving what its owner shot. The interloper tipped their head back to get a better look. Actual sunlight fought its way through fake foliage to light the face.

It was his mother.

Shocked, Guy was about to say "Mom?" Before he could, Ruthie turned and took off. At the same time, Guy's phone got a text. He scrambled in his backpack to retrieve it, losing his focus on the parent moving away. He saw who the text was from and what it said.

Where are U? Car company said you weren't there. Let us know. Worried. Mom

Guy returned home with trepidation. He'd removed what traces of actual or imitation nature had attached themselves to his clothes and skin. He wouldn't bother to lie; why should he when Ruthie already knew where he'd been? Yet how *could* she know? The text from his mother had come too close to her appearance in the woods. And it couldn't have been a timed message because she didn't know he would run away after my exam—because *he* didn't know! (And I'd told no one.)

Guy turned a corner in the house and bumped into her.

Ruthie wasn't dressed as she'd been in the park. She wore a dress, not a plaid shirt and cargo pants. Guy had never seen her in such a get up, anyway. She was always helplessly stylish, even just hanging around. Maybe it had been a disguise, a way not to get caught?

"There he is," Ruthie said, relieved.

Guy nodded, feeling sorry for disobeying (which was an instinct with her, like sneezing when dust went up your nose). Today the feeling didn't last, for he'd had a taste of escape and then had it weirdly, inexplicably curtailed. So, he felt resentful, too, and bewildered and a little bit afraid.

"Where did you go?" Ruthie asked.

Guy knew she was no actress. She truly didn't know the answer. None of it made sense.

"I just took a walk," he said, again responding by rote and immediately taking pity on her, as he always did when his mother showed concern. Yet his puzzlement, fear, and—even if it barely existed, I'll take credit for it—anger persisted.

"A *walk*?" Ruthie wasn't angry; she never was. As always, she was hurt and incredulous that she'd been hurt by *him*. "Why didn't you *tell* me? You know we would have been all right with that—if we'd known. But not to know…those minutes of anxiety have shorted my life, Guy. Doctors say they do."

Guy just nodded once more. He thought what she said was exasperating. His own life had been filled with the anxiety Ruthie claimed he had initiated in *her*—anxiety she and Magnus had been instilling in him for all of the ten years he'd been around. And now Ruthie had appeared at the exact same time she texted him, at the very second he had mildly and briefly evaded her and his father's attentions, something which was impossible.

Or had neither of his parents had anything to do with it? Had ten years of living with them simply conditioned him to create such a scenario in his head the second he stepped out of line? Had he merely *imagined* his mother, augmented her words of worry pulsing in his pocket, in order to punish and stop himself?

Guy was about to interrogate Ruthie, to ask where she had been that afternoon. But he both feared coming off as crazy and conceding that she and his father had *made* him crazy—he had his pride (or he'd developed some, after his appointment with me). Besides, at that moment, Magnus walked through the front door. Had his father been secretly watching from somewhere and planned this opportune entrance? Now Guy distrusted everything.

"What's going on?" Magnus asked, as if picking up on the tension in the air with sensors he had also installed.

"Nothing," Guy said, chickening out and chastising himself for doing it. "Nothing at all."

In the morning, Guy left for school early, grabbing the recycled container of organically grown vegan lunch from Ruthie's hand without a kiss or a thank you. He saw a driverless car waiting outside, paid for by the most privileged parents in the neighborhood to transport their kids. He approached it, oblivious to which of his own parents watched from the window.

"I'm walking today," he said, through the open car door to the kids on the shared seat, who gazed at him expectantly. Guy reached in and pressed the "Close Door" button, overriding the automatic response to his buttocks hitting leather. He walked, then jogged, then ran away again.

Guy had no destination in mind. As he had the day before, he was just compelled to disobey, addicted to it now; it was his ten-year-old's drug of choice. He knew there was nowhere to go, not in our town of Mossy Bend—flying was the physical action he wished hopelessly to achieve, for he felt trapped upon Earth.

Soon Guy found himself on the edge of town. Here he passed perplexed construction workers and entered a huge work site of new developments.

"Hey, kid!" he heard behind him. Guy realized it was a robot worker and didn't respond.

He walked on rock and gravel into a dangerous place on the verge of existing, an idea which he could not yet connect to himself. Feeling another presence at his back, he turned.

It was that woman again.

This time, she wore a fashionable outfit, a diaphanous dress with stick figure pelicans on it. Her head was dipped and her face obscured. Suddenly, another flash of light seemed to cue her to lift it.

Guy saw that it was Ruthie.

Guy had only been gone a few minutes and no car was anywhere to be found. Incensed—but more shaken—by her presence, he strode forward, his kicking sneakers sending plumes of soil into the air.

"Hey, how did you…"

His mother tried to flee, but Guy's surprisingly strong grip prevented her. He realized that the light illuminating Ruthie was not natural but man-made, not shining but projected. The person he believed to be his mother was a man with a hologram of his mother flickering on him, a living screen for Ruthie.

His name was Harry Taub. It wasn't hard for Guy to find out, because Harry immediately told him. He shrugged and sagged where he stood, seemed to shrink inside his neutrally colored suit (the best, he said later, on which to project an image). As Guy's hold loosened, the visual of his mother slid off Harry, shifting to the side like an old unspooling film, then shivering in the sooty air like a ghost before disappearing. The projector—hidden in one of the buildings being constructed or in a drone overheard—had been shut down, leaving Harry nude, as it were.

After saying, "Harry Taub," he extended a hand covered in blue dots, which also aided him in hosting the hologram. Guy didn't know what else to do but shake it. Harry's grip was weak, unlike his grasp on reality.

"I'm just an actor," he said. "It's just a gig. Sorry, kid."

Despite his casual attitude, Guy felt that Harry was upset about being discovered. After he stopped shaking Guy's hand, both his hands still shook.

"I'd offer to buy you breakfast," Harry said, "but a grown man eating with a little boy sets off the old alarm bells. You know?"

Guy didn't know, being ten and still an innocent (Ruthie and Magnus had made sure of it). Harry must have seen this as an advantage, for his face turned quizzical.

"Hey…" he said, "how come you're not in school?"

Was the question a way for Harry to deflect attention from himself? Guy was innocent not stupid.

"I *could* have breakfast," the boy said, starting a negotiation, trading one secret for another. "How about here, outside?"

Harry nodded, impressed by Guy. He pushed his lower lip into his upper, which made him look older, even ancient. Yet Guy thought it gave him gravitas, too.

"Smart kid."

They shared a genetically altered scone on a Mossy Bend sidewalk, near enough to the cordoned-off site that Guy felt his parents wouldn't drive by. Harry had taken the treat from his pocket, an act to the boy both magical and pathetic. Then Harry "chased" his own bites of the bread with sips from a flask he returned to his *other* pocket. Guy recognized the smell on Harry's breath from when his parents would kiss him goodnight after a party.

"Look," Harry said. "Work is scarce for a guy like me. So, I'm doing holograms."

"Did my parents hire you?" an emboldened Guy asked, licking his fingers, for the scone was so good.

Harry shrugged. "Probably. The offer came through my agency. But they gave me the backstory. 'Play parent and keep your eye on the kid.' You won't be my first kid and you won't be my last. But you're the only kid who's ever been clever enough to ask." He toasted Guy with the flask before tippling again.

Guy was both impressed and disturbed by Harry's drink breaks, by his physical condition in general. His nose was a map of busted blood vessels which led to badly chapped lips above white rice-like stubble. It was clear that he had not been altered in vitro to eliminate a hereditary propensity for alcoholism. (Guy may not have been able to put this into words, but I just did.) This meant that Harry was at an income level lower than Guy's family, which interested and upset the boy. Guy's anger at his family's persistent spying was morphing into another feeling, one both easier to handle and expanding his emotional palette. He felt empathy for this man paid to snoop.

"In my world," Harry said with a blearier shrug, "I take what comes along."

The older man's lack of security was in such contrast to his parents' obsession with the subject that Guy stared at Harry and hung on his every word, no matter how slurred they became.

"Of course, younger actors usually play the older parts," Harry said, expansively gesturing with the uneaten end of his scone. "They need more makeup but they have more energy and are less of an insurance risk."

Harry's next shrug dismissed the entire unfair world. When Harry found his flask empty, a little light went out of his eyes—natural light, not the man-made kind. Guy saw that no matter how he had gotten there or what had made him this way, the old actor, unlike himself (as I had pointed out), was free.

"Nothing's left," Harry said, sadly, holding the flask upside down. "See?"

Guy nodded. He took out his small wallet, the first he'd ever had. "Get some more." He pulled out his all-purpose payment card, which was linked to his parents' bank accounts.

"Nah." With an effort, Harry raised his white, curling, untamed eyebrows. "I won't get paid until the job is done. So, I couldn't pay you back."

"It's all right." Guy had learned the power of bargaining and introduced a new trade. "You can teach me."

"Teach you what?"

"What you know."

Harry stared at Guy with a bloodshot look that said, you care enough to ask me that? You respect me enough? And again the boy's understanding of life increased.

They stayed near the curb at the entrance to the construction site since Harry was being monitored and his agency would know if he left. He checked the ground to make sure it was safe to stand, stoop, and jump upon. As the noise of bulldozers, dump trucks, and drones continued in the near distance, Harry showed Guy the basics of dramatic movement. The boy followed as best he could, making sure the old drunk didn't fall, hit his head, and kill himself.

At the end of the morning, Guy had energy to burn, but Harry was exhausted. Sitting back on the curb, he snoozed. Then a truck backed up with a particularly loud beep and he snorted awake. Harry was confused as to where he was. Seeing Guy, he remembered.

"Okay," Guy said, holding up the payment card. "A deal's a deal."

"Keep it, kid," Harry lightly pushed aside the small hand. "Wait until we finish our lessons. We're just getting started."

"But…"

Harry wouldn't hear any more about it. Unsteadily, he stood and checked his watch. "I got another gig. You're not the only disobedient boy in Mossy Bend, you know."

By now, Guy was astute enough to know that Harry had insulted him so he wouldn't grow too attached. After all, Harry might be asked to "play" his parent again.

"And you're not the only ham," Guy said.

Harry did a double-take—a real one—reacting to the boy's quick-wittedness. An expression of parental pride crossed his face, then was shrugged away. Harry stumbled off down the road, waving only once, without turning around.

"Go to school!" he called. Then the words—like Harry himself—disappeared into the dust.

When Guy got home, he didn't mention seeing his "mother" that morning, and Ruthie didn't confront him about cutting school. Each simply acted as if neither thing had happened. This created a distance between them, the kind which had been more common in families of earlier generations, when parents and children had been less close. As opposed to feeling guilty or sorry, Guy simply could not wait until the next time he could skip school and see Harry Taub.

The next time he did, though, he was disappointed. Guy had slipped into an entertainment arcade and watched many five-minute superhero mini-epics (mepics, as the kids called them), enhanced by a virtual reality helmet. During the fourth hour, he'd become aware that someone had sat down several hundred rows behind him in the huge and—as usual—empty theater. He rose from his motorized spinning lounger to approach the person, hoping against hope that it was Harry.

After he proceeded up the endless carpet, he recognized the other as a phony version of his mother. But when he got close, he saw that this time Ruthie's hologram holder was a woman. Chagrined, Guy started to make the long march back to his seat.

"Wait," the woman said.

Guy turned back. Projected from somewhere in the theater, the image of Ruthie stayed exactly upon the woman's form, so it felt as if his mother addressed him. Yet the voice was older and tougher.

"You're Guy," she said.

Guy nodded.

"Harry couldn't come. I'm filling in."

"Is he all right?"

"Couldn't be better. He got a *real* gig today. He's playing an elderly villain in a special *six*-minute superhero picture. And he beat out younger people playing older to get it."

"Wow."

"He said to say you inspired him to go for it. He said, 'Tell that kid I've even quit drinking. While I'm working, anyway.' By the way, I'm Marjorie, his ex-wife. I hate his guts. But I'll still do him a solid."

The information was coming fast and furious—and was too adult for Guy to understand. He only got that something good had come from Harry "teaching him the ropes" and that Harry and his ex-wife were close enough to look out for each other. These were more mind-broadening ideas—there had been so many in the last week.

"Where is he?" Guy blurted out. "Can I see him? Where does Harry live?"

The image of his mother—the facial features quivering and breaking up—paused. Did Marjorie not want to divulge private information? Or, being an actress, was she hurt that Guy seemed not to care about *her*? (My guess.) Then she told him and Guy closed his eyes to memorize the address. When he opened them, the lights had fallen, everything was dark, and even the facsimile of his mother was gone.

The next day Guy cut school again and went to Harry's home. He covered his face with a hoodie, hoping that his image on his father's public cameras would be indistinct. He didn't notice figures following him, playing his parents or not. By lunch, he had reached the tiny apartment near the old abandoned light rail tracks.

Harry's home was just one room in the lobby of an apartment house, near where mops and buckets were kept; even Guy knew it had been a supply closet. The doorman didn't bother stopping Guy when he said whom he wished to visit, didn't care who came to see Harry. After knocking, through the door, Guy heard the dim sound of someone singing an obscene song.

"Harry?"

The voice shifted into an angry, phlegmy interrogative. "*What?*"

After Guy identified himself, nothing happened. So, he pressed unassertively on the door, which no one had fully closed. He saw Harry sprawled in a chair, wearing a sleeveless T-shirt, polka dot shorts, and support socks with garters. He was guzzling from a flask, staring and singing out the apartment's one small dirty window into an alley. His turn to perceive his guest was as slow and mechanical as that of a ventriloquist's dummy.

"Look who's here," he said.

"Hi." Even though he was ten, Guy knew the signs of adult dishevelment and, as an adult might, discreetly ignored them. "How did the job go?"

"How did the *job* go?" Harry mocked him, squeezing his features together in a parody of kissing. "How did the *job* go? Oh, it *went*, boy-o. It went!" Harry tipped the flask once more, but the container slipped from his sweaty fingers to the floor. Harry dropped and crawled after it, among discarded devices, food containers, and clothes. Finally, his reaching hand knocked it beneath his fold-out bed.

Harry cursed. On all fours, with makeup he hadn't removed seeping down his face, he spoke to Guy in a voice at once a whisper and a scream.

"They found out how old I was!" Harry said. "They said it was safer and cheaper to hire someone young to be old. I said I was the real thing, actually old. They said I was too big an insurance risk, too expensive. So, they canned me." He licked reflexively at the black paint dripping into his mouth. "This is your fault, you little rat. If you hadn't had faith in me, this never would have happened!"

Harry began scuttling towards Guy on his elbows and knees like a soldier evading bombs. Guy backed up, alarmed by the older man's advance and the crazed and furious look on his face. Right when he was about to reach Guy, his blemished fingers curling around his shoe, Harry passed out, his face upon the floor, his sparse and flyaway hair blowing in a breeze he'd made himself.

Guy learned the name of Harry's talent agency and went there in person. By now he knew that a crying child could get his way in the world. He forced himself to weep, "acting" in a way that would have made Harry proud. He got what he wanted, which was Harry's ex-wife Marjorie's contact information.

Marjorie was half-asleep when she answered the phone and half in the bag (I think). Guy turned on the tears again, begging her to help Harry, explaining that he had done what he could but Harry blamed Guy and wouldn't accept his aid. By the end of his entreaty, Guy was aware that his sobs were for real.

Guy returned to school. He told his parents nothing, not even that he knew how they had tailed and tried to control him and that he didn't love them anymore. He felt sure they knew *some* of this, but how far could they actually get inside his head? He vowed: not far and not any longer. From now on, he could at least hide from them in there.

At the end of the week, Guy rode home in the communal car. He casually looked over the shoulder of a classmate watching the latest mepic on her phone. He saw a superhero trying to save a beloved, dying old president, before killing in graphic detail the terrorists who had poisoned him after breaking into the oval office.

"May I?" he asked the girl. Engrossed, she refused to let him borrow her device until the story was done. Then Guy watched it from the start. When it was over, he pressed the emergency brake button and got out blocks before his home.

This time, Guy endured an interrogation from Harry's doorman. When insisting he was Harry's "friend" wasn't enough, he broke away and flew to the door.

Today it was shut. His incessant knocking and cries of "Harry!" eventually brought footsteps and the unsnapping of locks.

Marjorie stood in the threshold.

"Oh, good!" she said, "I thought it was the landlord again."

Guy peered past her. He saw a nearly empty room with packed boxes taking up most of the floor. The fold-out bed and the rest of the furniture were gone.

"First of all, kid," Marjorie said, pressing a balled-up tissue against her red and runny nose. "Thanks. Harry and I would never have had these wonderful days together without you. So, kudos, you know?"

Guy didn't recognize the ancient word for praise but, perceiving it was positive, he shrugged that it had been nothing.

"I saw Harry's new mepic," Guy said. "Did he go somewhere to work on another one? Is that where he is?"

Guy had heard that success could tear adults apart, creating distance due to new obligations or inflated egos. He wondered if this was what had happened and why Marjorie was so upset.

"No," Marjorie waved him away. "I encouraged the old fool to audition again, even when he didn't want to. He got cast as the dying president. When the producers found out how old he was, they wanted to fire him, of course. It turned out Harry was *actually* dying. That's why he was so good and got the part. By the time they tried to can him, he was dead. For real. It was his last hit."

Marjorie choked out a sob like a cough, pressing the fraying tissue harder against her nose. Guy had to strain to hear what she said next.

"They want us out of here today. Harry was behind on his rent, not surprisingly. I say 'us' because we recently re-married—after many drinks, I admit. But it still counts. Right? Because of you!"

Marjorie swiveled back around. To Guy's shock, she landed in his arms and her embrace was filled with grief, gratitude, and fear. He had never known one person could feel so many things at once. He held her as if to absorb yet another new idea. It was Marjorie who disengaged first.

"Anyway, he had a new hologram parent gig today. I better fill in. We—I mean, me, I mean, I—need the bread. I sure hope they can use an actress who cries."

Though she claimed to be in a hurry, Marjorie didn't move, seemed in fact paralyzed by being so bereft. Guy learned one more thing, this time about himself. He touched the older woman's arm to tell her.

Guy figured the assignment wouldn't be to follow *him*—that would be too perfect; life didn't work that way. Besides, he believed that his parents had stopped. He had seen no one behind him for ages. So, it would be someone else he would be pursuing.

Guy tried to remember what acting tips Marjorie had given him before he left the apartment. And he pledged to use everything Harry had taught him, too. He watched a disobedient girl, who was around Guy's own age. Guy stayed still and let the hologram find and flicker on him. The light was like all the new information that had illuminated him; all that knowledge fluttered onto and fit his frame.

The girl stood at a small distance from him in Mossy Trails. When she turned and saw Guy, she saw her mother. And at that moment, Guy felt he *was* Harry and would be Harry forever, for he had loved Harry and when you loved someone, you were never free, not really, and that was all right. And this was the most important and the last thing Guy learned before he turned eleven.

Doubles Alley

Journeyman Player on a New Journey…to Victory

By Brent Zahn

For years now, Boyd Melchior has been a likable player. This is arguably the   worst thing you can say about an athlete. He was a nice guy, someone who never pushed or offended, who tried just hard enough to do all right but never *that well.* His body, too, was nice—easily bruised and broken, lacking resilience and enough natural armor to keep him out of hospitals and off painkillers and crutches. Away from the tennis court, his demeanor was pleasant and polite. He was a guy everyone liked or maybe just never thought about enough to hate.

Now, at thirty, Boyd has been reborn.

For the past year, he's slashed and slammed; he's contested calls that were incontrovertibly true because a computer made them; he's used every stroke, including an obnoxious underhand serve; he's grunted loud enough to undermine his opponents; and when he's won, he's ripped off his shirt and pounded his chest.

He's been doing that a lot. Because he's been winning a lot.

His body has followed suit: He hasn't been hurt (even when running, sliding, and falling to reach every ball) or under the weather, no matter what bug is around.

Off the court, Boyd, well…how can I put it on a family Web site? He's been a total and utter SOB. Actually, that's too erudite a term. He's been a caveman, barreling past other people before and after matches, getting into fist fights and foul-mouthed arguments (though he says *much* less than he used to). Drug tests have found no pollutants in his veins; this has been a national evolution (or de-evolution, depending on your taste). Boyd's got a new agent—Tine Sochis, the top fellow in the field—but he doesn't have a coach. He's done it all himself.

If before, Boyd had slid into the hundreds in the rankings, now he's clawed his way back up into the high teens, an amazing ascension in such a short amount of time. And this weekend, he'll play in the finals of the U.S. Open.

How has this happened? We don't know.

All we know is that it's working.

So, all hail the new and improved Boyd Melchior! Then get out of the way of his serves and returns, his mouth and his fists.

Boyd read the article again on his device. It had been written by a top sports journalist who had never been anything but patronizing to him. At first, with the Open final tomorrow, he thought he'd been exposed. He was relieved it wasn't true. His secret, like his ranking, was safe.

Boyd could only have imagined what his father would have said—hollered, to be exact. His father had both pressured him to be a champion and made him skittish about being aggressive, made him shrink from the power that would have propelled him to the top. Had it been to punish his father—Lloyd Melchior, who'd named his son to rhyme with himself—that Boyd had always been promising and always fallen short?

God knows Lloyd had punished *him* enough. Years earlier, Lloyd had been described in a "Worst Tennis Dads" article that went viral as "all the world's nightmare tennis fathers rolled into one." They'd listed Lloyd's offenses in a funny ten best list, funny after the fact and to anyone but Boyd. Lloyd had:

In an Under-Ten Tournament, from the stands, loudly applauded Boyd's child opponent's double-faults and mistakes, and yelled "Kick him in the nuts!"

Made Boyd run home behind the car if he'd had what Lloyd believed was a bad practice

Beat him and shot at him with a BB gun if he lost as much as a set

Punched out two fans at a tournament who weren't "paying enough attention" to his son's match

Smashed journalists' phones at an after-party

Publicly accused organizers of fixing a draw

Had a violent tantrum about the price of crab cakes in a players' lounge, eventually upending a table

Broken the nose of Boyd's teenage practice partner by butting the boy in the head

Allegedly spiked the drinks of Boyd's opposing players, leading to one totaling his car afterwards and losing the use of his legs—though nothing was ever proven and Lloyd had denied it to Boyd's face

Been banned from attending any pro tournaments anywhere in the world.

A year ago, Lloyd had injected a liter of vodka into his veins (using a new process of drinking, the patent of which was recently approved) and dived into the pool of the hotel where he had tracked down Boyd, staying there under an assumed name to escape him. Lloyd fell head-first into the shallow end, hit the bottom and died immediately while other bathers (including children) at first laughed and then screamed.

After his death, Boyd had learned the truth about his father. Unsure from the start about Boyd's level of commitment and aggression, Lloyd had arranged to harness his enormous potential and perfect it. Secretly, with the ultra-sports agency, Swish, Spike, Slam, and Dunk (S, S, S & D), Lloyd had taken genetic materials from Boyd.

He had mixed and matched the levels of ferocity, until he finally mastered the recipe of male aggression. Then he had created a clone of his son.

Boyd learned this at the reading of Lloyd's will. Named Floyd, this new Boyd could perform any stroke and reach any ball. He could battle from the baseline or serve and volley; he could hit ace after ace. He could jam his opponent with a shot to the chest or toy with him by sinking a delicate lob and watch him run, pointlessly, to retrieve it. Most importantly, he never stopped fighting and ran everything down. He did not see aggression and winning as unfair to others, as Boyd did. He did not try to spite or disobey his "father" and lose. This was a version of Boyd with his mind removed or the part of his mind that had sabotaged himself. His double was—as he had been created to be—a champion.

Sadly, this other version of Boyd had limited language skills. S, S, S, and D and his dad had concentrated on Floyd's athletic ability and skimped on the intellect, favoring the brain power needed to play a game over reading skills and speech.

A contract had been drawn up in which Boyd would be secretly hired as Floyd's coach. He would be retained by the week, his rate of pay rising according to results (a certain amount if Floyd got into tournaments, higher if they were Majors, heavy "bumps" if he made the Finals or, best case, actually won). The arrangement would last five years, with an option to renew in two-year increments. What would happen to Floyd in the case of its dissolution was unstated and left to the discretion of the agency alone. The two men would move into the same apartment in New York City. Facing a career of unending mediocrity, his body ever collapsing, Boyd had signed.

Months before the Open, Floyd had played his first lower-tier tournament. It was one of many new Fan Fun events

("Fannies" or "Funnies," as they were nicknamed) that had relaxed rules of play, designed to take the elitism out of sport and attract younger crowds. They were laboratories for changes that could be made to the Majors which, like all public events, had been leaking audiences and money due to climate catastrophes, pandemics, mass shootings, and dirt-cheap home alternatives. (Once-popular mainstays like the World Series and the Super Bowl now allowed virtual reality participation by viewers and home voting on foul and strike calls.)

The Tarkofsky Crunch was a "Funny" or "Fanny" held in an ex-cattle stable in an Eastern European dictatorship. Boyd had stashed Floyd in his hotel room and arrived at the arena a day early to scope the place out. His agent at S, S, S, & D, Tine Sochis, told the organizers that Boyd had a head cold—"nothing serious, a little laryngitis"—so Floyd could avoid interviews. Snarky local reporters wrote that the "mediocre, oft-injured American was a surprise entry."

On his way in, Boyd ran into a familiar figure.

"Well, look who's still alive, sort of," Ole Millstrom said, in his unaccented English. He was a Swedish player who had mopped the court with Boyd every time they'd played. Ole stood in the sunlight, which poured on him like gold coins from a fairy tale.

"You playing here?" Ole asked with his usual smirk, the polluted sun glancing off his brilliantly blonde hair and reminding Boyd of how telegenic he was and how many endorsements he had (Ole was the face of the #1 self-driving car and the credit card tattoo). How he'd asked it sounded contemptuous.

"Yes, I'm playing," Boyd said. "You, too?"

"Me?" Ole said, with an incredulous expression that crinkled the impeccable skin beneath his piercing blue eyes. "Yeah, right."

"Then what are you…'

"The Tarkofsky's naming a court for me. I'm making a speech at the dedication. To inspire kids to play here. And, you know, older players who could use a break."

Boyd realized he had just left himself as open verbally as he had physically for most of their last match. He could have kicked himself.

When he turned to go, he snapped at Ole, "Hope it's hygge," meaning homey, and Ole called after him…

"That's Danish. I'm Swedish, you idiot!" which only made it worse.

The next day, when Floyd came out on court, the stands were half-empty and most spectators were attending for free. There were school kids on a field trip, residents of a mental institution, and soldiers on leave from a local base. Pets were allowed and—even though some were robotic—one could hear whines, barks, and even moos as Floyd warmed up. A DJ spun uncensored rap hits from yesteryear, encouraging sing-alongs from the crowd, often feeding them the obscene lyrics himself.

Like other "Fannies" and "Funnies," the Tarkofsky had new and generous court and equipment specs. Held on a self-cleaning hard surface made of hazardous materials, it boasted higher nets, wider courts, and balls which were six to eight percent bigger and made to bounce lower due to reduced internal pressure, guaranteeing more "goofballs and punchlines." Courtside computerized Auto-Coaching was prohibited, because it lacked "eyeball-stroking optics." Instead, actors dressed as coaches in black-and-white striped shirts and caps (nostalgic images so old no one alive could remember them) mimed and mouthed signals and frenetically danced to more rap blared during turnovers and between points.

The announcer was costumed as a forgotten idea of a reporter (wearing a fedora with a piece of paper reading "Press" perched on the brim) and held a cardboard microphone to his lips. Egged on by the DJ, the crowd both cheered and viciously mocked the display.

Floyd's opponent, Flac Lochshmire, was a Serbo-Croatian who had served time for match fixing and bribed his way out of prison to get back on tour. His incarceration had left him tattooed over most of his body, including racist epithets scrawled on his face. When Floyd saw him across the net, he laughed, which earned a threatening sneer from Flac. Floyd imitated it, witheringly, and the intoxicated crowd roared.

Floyd had never played for an audience. At first, he stared at them with fascination and fear. Then it became clear they had inspired him to ratchet up his show.

"Let's go!" he yelled, surprising both Flac and the umpire, a large child picked by lottery from the crowd.

The match was best of three with severe time limits for serving and crossovers, as well as no bathroom breaks (buckets were placed on either side of the net). While the amateur umpire was given nominal power over contested points, the crowd had final say, which it exercised by bellowing "in" or "out."

Yet there was no contesting what happened in the first set. Floyd won every point of his service games with aces, never even approaching the net. Twice his ball hit the lines so perfectly and so hard that the burst of flying paint dust blinded his opponent. Receiving, he broke Flac's serves easily and with no less brutality. He mocked the waddling gait and wiggling breasts of the flabby parolee, who had over-indulged on prison grub and spent no time in the facility's gym.

Floyd's power game, plus his heedlessly aggressive behavior, so rattled Flac that when he lost—0-6, 1-6—he made to fling his racket at him before he bounced it disgustedly off the ground. As he left the court, he called to the clone in Serbo-Croatian, words obviously curses and threats of retribution.

Boyd had watched the match on the TV in his room. While the commentary was un-translated, he could tell that those covering the match had been both impressed and shocked by Floyd's display.

"This was a new Boyd Melchior," one said, in halting English.

When Floyd returned to their room, he was—in the old expression—bouncing off the walls. He shadow-boxed an imaginary enemy, then flung his fists at Boyd, who caught and held them still.

"Knock it off," he said.

"I won!" Floyd yelled.

"I know. And it's over."

"I won! Me!"

Floyd pulled free and danced around the room, again like a boxer. He sent out jabs and roundhouses—and overheads and volleys, sticking to his own sport—breaking picture frames, flower vases, and drinking glasses.

"Stop," Boyd said. "That's enough!"

Boyd knew that, like a wild animal, Floyd needed more room to roam than the cramped Eastern European hotel suite. He had no choice.

"Get your coat," he said. "We're going out."

Boyd pulled a cap with the S, S, S, & D logo over his face. He pushed his hands deep into the pockets of an agency wind breaker. Bounding beside him, Floyd was so invigorated by his victory that he flung his coat over a guardrail into a river.

Boyd kept them to the back streets, out of the way of tourists, the indiscreet or merely curious. Still, he couldn't avoid everyone in the small but well-populated foreign city.

Floyd sensed him stiffen at the approach of a group of men.

"Who?" he asked.

"I don't know," Boyd said.

"Friends?"

"Maybe."

When the three came close, Boyd could see that they were indeed not friends. Two were well-muscled beneath their long, leather, Soviet-style overcoats. The man in the middle was short and plump, wearing a light, tacky polyester vest. A tiny oval of his face was visible under his own woolen cap. Boyd could see that tattooed foreign words decorated his cheeks, nose, and brow.

"Flac Lochshmire," Boyd said.

"What?"

Boyd realized the clone had never known the name of the man he'd beaten and couldn't have cared less.

"The player," Boyd said, quickly, for the three were advancing, "who you…"

"Oh." Floyd got as close as he could to a giggle.

Boyd made a mental note: "Teach good sportsmanship" at their next coaching session. Then he didn't know if they'd ever reach it.

"Loser!" Floyd called. "Hey, loser! Hi, loser!"

Steps away, the trio came to a sudden stop. Flac tipped his head toward his companions, who were obviously his bodyguards. Even with much of his face obscured, his expression was legible: Get a load of this guy.

"You!" Floyd repeated. He re-ran his imitation of Flac's funny walk, which had been such a hit during the match.

Flac stared, incredulous that Floyd was still pulling this stuff. He seemed spooked by the extent of the clone's insensitivity. Illuminated by a streetlamp, fear flashed in the other man's eyes. Then he regained confidence. Flac flicked the arms of his tougher companions, signaling them: Come on.

As he plugged forward, Flac briefly checked out Boyd. He was relieved that the visible piece of *his* face didn't identify him. The three moved swifter than Boyd was expecting.

"Uh oh," Boyd said.

"What?"

"I'll cut right. You cut left. We'll meet back at the hotel."

"Go?"

"Yes. Go. Obviously."

"Okay. Go." Floyd meant, you go. I'm staying. Obviously.

"You're kidding, right?"

"Right." Floyd was being sarcastic, a first for him. Had he always been able to do that? Or did the clone only learn what he wanted to learn? Far from fleeing his aggressors, Floyd was powering toward them. Boyd exited stage right, yelling…

"Don't be crazy! Come on!"

But Floyd kept going.

It didn't happen the way it did in movies, with the hero dispatching one foe after another with ease. Instead, Floyd barreled into Flac Lochshmire like a baby cannonballing another baby, for fun. When two piled on Floyd to protect the third, and real pain started being induced, Floyd was still having a good time.

"Knock it off!" Flac yelled in his own tongue. Floyd was hammering on him as the two strongmen struggled to tear him off. The clone elbowed the first in the face while kneeing the second in the groin.

"That's enough!" Boyd whispered from a safe place on the sidewalk, in the shadows.

"Soon!" Floyd responded, as one of Flac's cronies, the one who'd been elbowed, sprawled backwards and the other, who'd been kneed, fell forward. Flac remained erect, and he was too scared not to run, which he did.

"Okay!" Floyd said to Boyd. "Now! Done! Coming!"

After the fisticuffs, Boyd saw that Floyd was sated and satisfied. Back home in the States, he even began to sleep without his usual night light. Boyd decided to forego fruitless attempts to harness the clone's violence and to secretly release it—off the court.

He knew that wear and tear on Floyd's appendages had to be kept to a minimum. So, he had to teach Floyd to keep the carnage brief, to run before he could be caught and not to be clocked in the face or kicked in the shins.

"Mostly menace them," Boyd advised.

"What's 'menace'?"

"It's when you…" Boyd had to resort to pantomime. In their apartment, he stalked the clone like a monster, teeth bared and arms extended, lumbering as if his legs were connected by screws and not bone. Floyd backed up, feigning fear, laughing like a horrible little boy.

Just as Boyd reached him (and was planning to pull away), Floyd got him by the neck and then the throat. The clone's fingers began to press.

"Stop," Boyd said, before Floyd's thumbs ended his ability to speak.

Floyd did stop, though he didn't take his hands away, just quit moving them. He held Boyd as you might a ladder climbed by someone you loved. Boyd stared at him, colors falling from his face, knowing that if he failed to police him now, he would never succeed. Boyd looked into the clone's eyes which were his own and knew that if he died, they would both cease to exist (in his case, literally). And suddenly, Floyd knew it, too.

He let Boyd go.

"Only menace," Floyd said.

Boyd hacked, coughed, and stumbled away. This had been the first time Floyd had acted on him physically. Boyd believed it would be the last.

Floyd steadily progressed on court until he burst through all speed stops, as it were, leaving his opponents in the dust. He won every "Fanny" and "Funny" he entered, treating each event (and most of its participants) with contempt. In ATP tour matches—from Acapulco to California to Brisbane—he reached the quarters three times, the semis in two and the finals in one, which he only lost in a tie break.

Floyd had no trouble qualifying for the Majors, where his results were remarkable—the quarters in Australia (before it was canceled due to climate change forest fires), the Round of 16 in the French (Floyd enjoyed sliding on the clay so much he sometimes forgot to hit the ball), the semis at Wimbledon (where even though the dress code had been relaxed to bolster young people's interest, Floyd's T-shirt featuring obscenities—unvetted by Boyd—got him into a screaming fight with the computerized Auto-Umpire and almost expelled), and, at last, the final of the U.S. Open.

Now Boyd saved the article on his device. He could only hope for the best in the match tomorrow.

Floyd's opponent would be Ole Millstrom.

When Boyd told him, the Swede's name meant nothing to Floyd, who had never seen him play. Ole, of course, knew Boyd. The next day, before the match, he stopped by the clone's locker.

"So, Boyd," Ole said, "good for you."

"Huh?" By now Floyd could use a few more words yet— Boyd was convinced—he just didn't feel like doing it.

"I said, good for you." Coming from Ole, even a compliment sounded like an insult.

"For what?" Floyd said,

"For improving so much. Is it being with S, S, S, & D?" The condescension would have been clear to anyone else.

Having no history with Ole, Floyd shrugged the remark away. Ole came to the sudden conclusion that Boyd seemed not to *remember* him, which was weird.

"Well," Ole said, not wanting to fill his head with what was weird before a match (despite Boyd's recent string of successes, Ole believed it was a fluke and about to be snapped), "see you out there."

"Where?" Floyd didn't even know this was the guy he was about to play.

This question was *too* weird for Ole. He left, suspecting Boyd was on a drug which had made him both win and weird. It was a suspicion he maintained for a few minutes and—he admitted later, in a press conference—distracted him at the top of the match.

Some matches are decided *at* the top—one player dominates, the other submits. Some matches go back and forth, with each player surging and fading. The U. S. Open final featuring Floyd and Ole was the first disguised as the second.

Ole won the toss and chose to serve. At first, Floyd sprayed returns from the baseline and stormed the net, hit balls harder than necessary, and generally displayed a lack of discipline destined to do him in. Yet in fact the match was over as soon as the next game started, when Floyd's titanic first serve spun the Swede around in a fruitless attempt to return. From then on, the mistakes Floyd made came either from capriciousness (he was experimenting with bad shots because he could afford to fool around and recover) or miscalculation (of how much force he needed from the frightening amount he possessed). In other words, Floyd could afford to be wrong once in a while because he was right so often. And he was still fiddling with the amounts of power in him as those inventing him had fiddled with his DNA. Ole didn't know any of this until it was too late.

"In!" Floyd screamed at one point, while his overhead still fell. The impertinence infuriated Ole right as he saw it land on the line, winning Ole the first set. This made the Swede realize he was going to lose and had been going to lose the whole time.

"Cheater!" Ole howled at the net when it was over, in lieu of a handshake (Floyd never offered one, win or lose; Boyd didn't know if he didn't comprehend the custom or didn't care). As the two exited, Ole barreled by and bashed into Floyd, knocking him off balance.

"Don't take the bait!" Boyd yelled at his screen at home. He was relieved to see that Floyd didn't retaliate, instead found his footing and mocked Ole's pigeon-toed progress into the locker room. The imitation angered the Swede more than any violence, since *that* might have revealed insecurity and a caricature came from confidence. Ole officially comprehended he had just lost in a final to Boyd Melchior, of all people, who had played with pitiless and awful brilliance.

Afterwards, Boyd and Floyd moved into the dark streets of New York, Floyd like a dog desperate to lose its leash. Boyd pulled his cap down especially low, for even these back alleys were lighted.

"Where? Where?" Floyd asked.

"Soon," Boyd said.

Boyd knew where to find gangs squatting in the barren landscape that had been the retail hub of Soho before the pandemics, looting, and floods. Here was where the hippest clothing and housewares had been sold and now the addicted, insane, and criminally cruel were harbored.

"*Where?*"

"Somewhere…there."

Miscreants had emerged from the murky and deserted dead end into which Boyd and Floyd turned. As soon as he saw them, the clone's head snapped back, like that same dog sniffing something delicious.

Boyd backed off, as he always did, seeking a doorway or alcove that would shield him from view and harm. Floyd ran ahead, like—yes, again—a dog at the run after a week of waiting. This dog wanted to do more than bound around and blow off steam. He wanted to spill some blood or at least do some damage.

"Hey!" Floyd yelled.

"What?" one of the gang members shot back, starting a fire in a garbage can.

"Knock it off!"

"Who says?"

"Me!"

Tonight, Floyd had met his match in inarticulateness. Even though his foe was backed up by pals eager to assist, the clone didn't mind and advanced.

Boyd hid his face behind his hands and pulled his hat down farther, to cover his ears. The muffled and obscured sights and sounds reminded him of old cartoons Floyd liked, fists and feet coming out of a cloudy circle of smoke.

After the melee, Floyd barely made it to bed before he fell asleep. He had won his first Major, then done maximum damage to others and minimum damage to himself, suffering no more than a scratch. Boyd watched him sleep like the most indulgent parent in the world.

Beside him in his own bed, Boyd too felt elated, filled with and drained of the same adrenaline. In the street, Boyd couldn't tell if the clone's moans of pleasure had been his own. For the first time, he had been too excited to care.

In Person

I don't know why she wore perfume. It didn't make any sense; he couldn't have smelled her. Yet if it put her at ease or even excited her, why not?

After all, it was like someone's wedding night in the old days, or so I would imagine. So many obsolete rituals had returned that maybe even that one—the commingling of virgins, the bride ignorant of intimacy, the groom waving the bloody sheet afterwards—might be coming back, too.

In any case, Saffron had arrived at this moment—the first sexual encounter with the young man who'd been courting her—through a conventional, one might even say conservative, route. The first step had been the traditional introduction by an older friend or relative, in this case, Saffron's Aunt Raveen, in whose four-story, rent-controlled apartment house on Washington Square the young woman lived (Saffron was either twenty-eight or twenty-nine, I'm not sure). Aunt Raveen had been alerted to this available male prospect by someone else, though when Saffron asked who it had been, her aunt—increasingly vague about everything—searched her mind and came up blank.

"It was—oh, someone told me, I can't remember who. Someone referred him to me, referred Cornelius to me and so to you."

Saffron knew that in her idle loneliness her elderly aunt often mistook mass emails requesting money for messages from friends, as she did similar texts and phone calls—another archaic custom making a comeback. So, Saffron wanted to make sure.

"I mean, you actually *knew* the person who recommended him, right?" she asked.

"Knew? As opposed to what?"

Her aunt's voice had risen to a register that meant she was both offended by what was being intimated and afraid it might be true. It made Saffron back off, from pity if nothing else.

"It's okay. Never mind."

"So, he may contact you? Cornelius?"

"Um—well—okay—of course—why not?"

Saffron's response had shot from uncertainty to indifference to enthusiasm and finally to a fiercer, freer form of indifference in which she cast care to the wind as opposed to abandoned interest in her life. She realized that she had done it as much to help herself as spare Raveen's feelings. Saffron wanted to believe an acceptable young man might be interested in her, for she was lonely living with just her aunt a flight up, even if she couldn't say the word, in the same way well-bred women once again avoided vulgarities.

"Good!" her aunt said, oblivious.

So, it began as courtships customarily did now, with an email (physical letters were forbidden). In it, Cornelius gave basic information about himself: He was thirty, 5'11", dark-haired. He worked as a forensic librarian, which he was able to do online and at home now that animated recreations of cells, specimens, and germs had been perfected and could replicate the real thing. Perhaps fearing that his profession might make him seem cold or dull, he joked that...

"Whenever I fear that *I* might be a recreation, too, I look in the mirror and..."

…he embedded a selfie taken in a bathroom mirror right after a shower. Cornelius had rubbed out a circle in the glass so that he appeared as in a cameo on a locket in another century or a circular "iris" that captured an image to end a silent film.

Saffron saw a man much more attractive than she would have imagined. His hair was not just dark but lushly, animal black, whipped away from his face by water, his eyes a midnight shade of brown, the rising steam in the room like hot vapor off a jungle river or something else uncivilized—she couldn't put it into words. In the oval made by his soapy hands, his shoulders were bare. The portrait made Saffron suddenly both chilled and overheated, as if she were nude in the bathroom with him or in the vegetative tropics or someplace else suffocating, dangerous and warmer than her nondescript (if immaculately kept) one-bedroom.

When Saffron scrolled farther down, she saw that Cornelius was still using the same polite, mildly humorous tone with which he had begun.

"If you'd care to write me back," he said, "I'd be very pleased to receive your letter. Warmly…" and he signed off with his full name, Cornelius Bellow.

Saffron waited for a while, her legs damp and sticking a little to the leather seat of her swivel chair. How should she respond and when? Right away? Or would that be desperate? Would waiting be coy or cute or, worse, make her seem blithe or even uninterested? She was new to this, so she didn't know.

Saffron decided she would answer immediately, but only after she had crafted a reply to her satisfaction; she wouldn't merely move her fingers upon the keyboard, which had also been made slippery by her sweaty hands. Using old-fashioned implements—pen and paper—she wrote draft after draft, attempting to find the best way to describe herself and what she did (Saffron was an online children's librarian, which was an incredible coincidence, though she filed books and not facsimiles of human effluvia and remains). She successfully copied Cornelius' breezy yet formal style and was stopped only by the prospect of providing a photo, as he had done.

Saffron was attractive—reasonably, anyway, if a tad mousy, she admitted, but maybe that was just the way she presented herself? She kept her blonde-ish hair in a bun, used no makeup, and wore formless, unbelted dresses, creating an effect of old-school cliché spinster mixed with severe young, cloistered novitiate, again comparisons that had not been made recently in the world. She knew she couldn't compete with Cornelius' startling shower snapshot, so she stood dressed before her bathroom mirror and the room was dry. The best she could do was literally let down her hair—which, finally free, exploded out, caressing her shoulders and brushing her breasts before swinging below her waist and landing in her lap. Her framed face now seemed very young, exposed, and unblemished except by freckles, which looked as naked as someone else's nipples, she thought. The mirror needed cleaning and had pops, pockmarks, and smears which made it appropriately like an artifact, a daguerreotype or whatever old photos had once been called. Saffron took the picture before she could reconsider.

Then she returned to her laptop and attached it to the body of her email, the way she might have planted a kiss on someone as he slept. She pressed "send," her finger staying on the key as a cartoon character's hand pressed a plunger to detonate dynamite. The email sailed away, a little boat striking out onto the sea…or another idea from days gone by in a world she and most other people would never know, due to the rampaging disease that had changed everything and forced them to always stay indoors, away from other people.

Saffron waited impatiently for her suitor's reply. She waited the rest of the day and into the early evening. Was Cornelius holding off as she had, not wanting to seem too eager? (Actually, she had only held off as long as it took to write the letter, which had been, what, an hour? Two?) Maybe he was busy collating or collecting something forensic, *working* in other words, as Saffron was not: she'd blown off her assignments ever since she'd heard from him. Who would ever know? It was an honor system for those who worked from home, which was almost everyone now.

Then Cornelius answered.

"I was delighted to receive your letter," he began and continued in the same courteous yet unpompous vein. He, too, marveled at the similarity of their jobs yet pooh-poohed Saffron's devaluing of her own in regard to his.

"I may cull and categorize things of the body," he wrote, "but you fill the minds and hearts of the young—places already mysterious—with what is truly intangible, the joys and insights of art. Who's to say which has more value?"

At the end, he inquired whether he might call her on the phone, which would officially take their relationship to the next stage, and this time Saffron did not hesitate at all before agreeing.

This wasn't when she put on perfume, but she did the next best thing: changed into a form-fitting and flowery dress. Saffron must have felt if she was surrounded by—her skin actually touching—a flattering fabric, her verbal expressions might follow and become more appealing. She feared that her voice was flat and rugged: she could hear a similar quality when her aunt spoke and Raveen was her only living relative, so the only evidence that it might be hereditary (though Raveen's voice was additionally ravaged by age). Saffron heard it when she told her aunt what happened.

"Oh, that's wonderful," Raveen said, safely over the phone, though she lived just steps away. "When is the call with you two?"

"Tonight." (This was a day later.)

"Just wonderful!"

Saffron was annoyed by her aunt's excitement. The old woman sounded as if she had heard that Saffron's biopsy result was benign when she'd assumed her niece was on death's door. Was her situation *that* desperate? Also, the way Raveen said "you two"—it was as if she and Cornelius were already a couple, and they'd only exchanged letters. Still, when she got off the phone was when Saffron changed clothes, feeling the pressure and perhaps a fear of her continuing insignificance if she kept living alone as a virgin.

Cornelius' voice was anything but flat and rugged when he got on the line. It was the aural equivalent of his picture: he seemed to speak through an undulating mist of dizzying hot spray from some kind of exotic spring in which he and she had stripped naked—Saffron didn't have the words because she'd never been to such a place and barely read enough to even imagine it. She heard his sounds—grunts, cries, and caws from jungle birds—before she made out his words, which were as they had been in print: mild, formal, and inoffensive.

"I hope you had a productive day."

"Me?" Saffron asked, helplessly injecting honesty and humor (and later feeling he'd been glad for it allowed him to do the same). "Productive would be giving me a lot of credit."

Cornelius laughed and his bird call became a mating trill, lyrical and instinctive, above and between branches. "Maybe it's good not to credit yourself and let other people do it. That's an old-fashioned quality and a good one."

"It might just be insecurity." Was she hoping to be contradicted or merely to be known by him? Saffron wasn't sure, so of course he couldn't be, either.

"Maybe," he said. "We'll see."

"Will we?"

No hesitation. "I hope so."

This deliciously vague exchange—or so Saffron found it—told her all she needed and slightly feared to know. She was very bad at picking up signals for, of course, in this world, few had ever been dropped for her. Yet Cornelius was scattering clues like feed in that forest, drawing creatures to him—and she decided to interpret them unambiguously, as if he had invited her to approach. Inevitably she was reminded, at least subconsciously, of other materials sprayed by excited male animals, though she had only ever seen photos and footage of such a thing in her secluded life, which was the life of everyone not wishing to die from deadlier essences now exuded by people.

"So?" she said, slightly breathless when there was a break in their conversation. She didn't need to say more; it was his turn.

"So," he said, and the word seemed to have different properties coming from his mouth, which was exciting. "I think we've…well, I've enjoyed this."

She saw no point in pausing. "Me, too."

"May I call on you?"

Saffron had hoped this question was coming and thought at least a few seconds of silence afterwards was appropriate, though not much more.

"Yes," she said, finally, and added—not as an imploration, which would make her pathetic—to be polite, a kind of conduct which had also returned to the world, for good or for bad, like an old plant popping up again after eons because soils had been stripped of pollutants, "please."

Cornelius could not call on her in person, of course. He would have to do it on computer, Saffron allowing him "in" by pressing a key that would have unlocked a downstairs door in a different day.

This was still pre-perfume. Yet Saffron did more than merely change her dress: she cut—or tried to cut—her own hair, an act she had never performed yet knew that people less graceful than she often had. She found she lacked both the manual dexterity and spatial sense for the task. Her hair fell like leaves in that tropics to the shore of which Cornelius would swim, dropped like the drawers of women who dived in with him—she couldn't stop dreaming of it—then piled up like poop laid by the ugliest animals in the area. Her head was left so straggly and uneven that she had to cover it with a cap, after failing to competently comb or pin it. She hoped it might seem "kooky" and not the manifestation of inner chaos, the "tell" that she was insane.

"I can see you. Can you see me?"

Cornelius said this when he came onscreen, the camera showing just his Adam's apple, shirt collar and a few strands of black chest hair wriggling like reeds at the bottom of that jungle lake.

"I can see some of…" she started to say, but the camera self-corrected and rose to reveal Cornelius' face.

Here, again, he appeared to lean in and out of smoke as actors once effortfully found the lens in 3-D films. Having more of her senses engaged—seeing and hearing him at the same time, his face and voice not separated as if by the official edict that had parted people—startled Saffron. It was a forceful reminder of the absence of other senses—touch and smell—in her life.

"Now I can see everything," she said.

"Good."

"Here."

A virtual bouquet of roses appeared in the top right corner of the screen. While Saffron could have pressed the "aroma" button, she declined, knowing from unpleasant experience involving food and not flowers—spaghetti marinara and don't get her started—its "smell" would be nauseating, an innovation that had been brought to market too early and still needed work.

"Thanks," she said. "They're lovely."

"I like your cap."

Instinctively, her hand went to her head, to either secure or remove it, she wasn't sure which, and her smile became a wince.

"Really?"

"Yes. It looks…kooky."

While this had been the effect she'd sought, hearing Cornelius confirm it—struggle to say it, as if it were new slang spread only among the young (which underscored either his mild fuddiness—an endearing quality in one so attractive as long as it stayed mere fuddy and didn't become full-blown fuddy-*duddiness*) made Saffron regret having worn it. Why create just one character when she wished to be known completely and always by him? Saffron bent forward and let the cap slip from her head the way tap dancers had once doffed top hats down their arms and elbows. Her patchy scalp filled the screen, looking like an aerial view of a battlefield being bombed.

"Ah," Cornelius said.

"That's why."

"Okay. I get it."

Had he cut his own hair? Up close and in real time, it looked as full, beckoning, and dark as in his photo.

"I did it for this," she blurted out. "For you."

This was a huge risk—and perhaps a foolish one, Saffron was aware. Why admit to anything negative at this point? Why not keep up all illusions until she was sure he was snared, or whatever was the right word? Yet she had barreled ahead because if she couldn't trust him with everything, with all of her, why bother? That's how much she wanted it.

"Well, you didn't have to," he said. "You don't have to do anything differently. Not with me."

And that kicked off the rest of their conversation. In earlier days, they might have emptied cup after cup of coffee but neither drank anything and Saffron only excused herself once to pee, which she might have done many times before.

In that other time, too, it might not have been wine they were drinking, not yet, that might have happened on the second date. And in fact, the next time they talked, each held something intoxicating (she wine, he beer) and by the third time, both had drunk an enormous amount.

Every time, their connection deepened—even as the one literally linking their computers faltered, freezing one's if not the other's face unflatteringly. A pattern emerged: she was voluble, he was quiet; yet she wasn't out of control but naturally emotional, and he wasn't icy but compassionate and good-humored. They balanced each other out: he was the matchbook that kept her table leg from leaning, she was the window flung open to air out his musty attic, or other references to rooms and restaurants they had never and would never be in. Suffice it to say, encouraged, both knew they were approaching an event in which words would either be unneeded or shouted and whispered as requests or orders either consensually obeyed or countermanded, whichever would be most exciting. Both knew the next time they saw each other, it would be different.

Saffron didn't want anyone else to know.

"How is it going?" Aunt Raveen asked, Saffron cursing herself for answering her call (she hadn't for a while).

"How is what?" she asked, too clever for her own good.

"You know what—I'm not an idiot."

Once again, her aunt resented being patronized or mollified simply because her mind was collapsing.

"Sorry," Saffron said and *was* sorry. "I'm just…it's hard to put into words."

"I know what *that* means," Raveen interjected, again revving up Saffron's and Cornelius' relationship in a way that irritated Saffron (though later she wondered if the old woman wanted her niece "taken care of" not because she feared Saffron might otherwise be alone forever but because she wished this issue resolved before her fading faculties vanished altogether).

"Yes," Saffron said, to be kind. "You do know. You're so right."

Saffron didn't tell her what was about to occur. How could she? It would be inappropriate. Yet Raveen (like many older women who had actually been physically married and widowed before everything fell apart) knew way more than Saffron would ever know. "Do yourself a favor," her aunt said.

"What?"

"Put on a little perfume."

This was when Saffron applied it. Did she do it as a dainty tribute to her aunt, a way to keep her disappearing period of history alive? Or had she done it for herself so she'd feel sensual, physical, and fleshy? Was she trying to experience her own organs, pores, and cells as she never had? Or was it a fantasy that he, Cornelius, might take her in as she took in herself, even though the program that let her sniff his roses didn't really work? I don't know: I only know what happened next.

Saffron and Cornelius faced each other through the screen and made love in the only way that people could now—by touching themselves while watching the other. Saffron made sure to wear something she could unbutton, for the prospect of yanking a dress down or up and over her head and possibly getting it stuck in her hair—not her hair, she had too little of it left, on something else—mortified her. She wore the old white blouse for which she settled while doing laundry. She hoped that its lack of color might be erotic for it suggested—not purity, as it had in dresses in weddings in other centuries—absence, the idea that she was a page eager to be illustrated, that he could spill and rub his color on her and they could create a new compound color, a complexion that hadn't existed before they did together.

Whatever, Saffron thought: she wouldn't be wearing the blouse for long. After they both stroked their faces as if caressing the other's and both stuck out their tongues as if tasting the other's (laughing at first for they felt like kids "flipping off" each other in the only way they knew how), both began to remove their shirts. Each stopped, to politely allow the other to proceed, which again made them laugh, for their "after you; no, after you" seemed silly under the circumstances. Then Cornelius quickly pulled off his sweater and T-shirt in order to let her take more time, which Saffron did, revealing the best black bra she had, which she also undid and removed, pressing her arms against her small breasts both to shield them and spread them out in a way she thought he would want, having seen enough old TV shows and films to know.

"Let me see you," he said, and his words were like his hands taking her arms down, which is what she herself did next.

Then Saffron touched herself, imagining his hands by looking in his eyes through the screen that separated them, aware that she would never know what they were like, that her hands would have to *be* his, just as his hands were hers as he jerked down his jeans and took his penis out. The camera was up too high to catch him and—surprising herself—Saffron, too, said:

"Let me see you."

He obeyed her as she had him, tipping the laptop down so it would show him holding his hard-on in his—her—hand.

Then her underwear was off and her right hand was between her legs, while the left stayed at her breasts. Even though she knew it was impossible, Saffron felt it was his fore and middle fingers inside her, insisting and retreating, while his thumb flicked her clitoris, his other hand tugging and rolling her nipples while her hand traced the stiff length of his penis, her wrist purposefully placed against his pubic hair so he'd feel it. She could see the spray of his semen, which he tried but failed at the last second to direct away from the screen, where it spattered like white rain, and she came, too, her cunt clamped around his thick fingers, his thumb smearing her clit like a painter dabbing a circle of that new color on her canvas again and again. The picture froze, immortalizing what his face looked like when he was at a peak of pleasure, and this is what their first time together ("going all the way," as they used to say, "going the distance," as they said now)—their wedding night—was like, wonderful in its way, for it was the only way they would ever know.

Afterwards, it took a while for the internet connection to come back. Cornelius was replaced by a black screen while the computer rebooted. Sitting exhausted in her swivel chair, Saffron held her clothes against herself for some reason. Maybe she was feeling vulnerable, exposed in a new way, that her own security system had been disabled or something. With Cornelius gone, she experienced a weird fear that he had never existed at all or, if he had, he was never coming back. Saffron had never had sex before and had known so little about it that she sensed a kind of post-coital panic.

Yet the panic was also positive: she felt a dizzying desire to do it again. Soon Saffron learned that Cornelius felt the same way, wanted it as much as she did. The next time they got together in their different apartments, they placed their hands against their screens—like prisoners and loved ones had once done on visiting days—and each began undressing using the other's hands, using their imaginations, which were as much a part of these encounters as the parts of their bodies.

"Maybe it was always this way," Cornelius said, dandling his hand against his chest hair as if parting the overgrown grass in their jungle—and his sweat had made it doubly dark.

"What was?" Saffron asked, as one, two, three of her fingers found her opening and liquid spilled from it onto her skin like a monsoon in the same place.

"I mean, maybe people always used their imaginations when they made love."

"Oh. Maybe."

"Just not as much as us."

"Right."

Then, naked from the waist down, Saffron stood, half-turned, spread her legs, and sat several times onto those fingers, which were as long and fat as she'd seen his penis to be. Cornelius had never glimpsed this side of her before: sweat had made the light line of hair on her spine rise like a new path leading them deeper into what was sweltering, stinking, and unexplored.

The next week, they were engaged.

Cornelius' ring was virtual like the roses, and when Saffron "accepted" the offering, the twirling diamond icon remained on the bottom corner of her screen.

"Marriage," of course, merely meant they would live together remotely—though substantial upgrades to their internet connections would be allowed once they had obtained (by email) the license. Additional and more arduous approvals would have to be granted for her to receive his sperm sample so they could try to reproduce. Saffron didn't want to think about that, not yet, partly because she didn't know if she wanted children or could even have them. She just wanted to appreciate this event for now. She had nearly given up on its ever happening.

And she knew whom to thank.

"What?" Aunt Raveen said, either because her phone or her hearing was faulty.

"I said, thank you."

"You're welcome." An unintentionally comic beat. "For what?"

Hadn't Saffron just said? She started to doubt her own cognition. "I'm engaged."

"Oh. *That's* what you said. I thought you said enraged."

Saffron laughed. Yet she knew people sometimes attributed their own discomforting emotions to others. Why would Aunt Raveen be enraged? Sympathetically, she turned the question around. "Why would I be enraged?"

"You tell me."

This was going nowhere. Luckily (or unluckily, as it turned out), Raveen now steered the discussion.

"Well, congratulations. It's what I was hoping for."

"Thanks." And Saffron gave her the benefit of the doubt for being so relieved.

"He's such a nice man."

"He is." How would *she* know? "You've talked to him?"

"And so humble. I mean, he didn't have to be so grateful."

"For what?"

"For what I gave him. I mean, who wouldn't have done it, under the circumstances?"

Saffron didn't want to keep questioning, yet she knew that—like many diminished people—her aunt enjoyed knowing more than someone, for it gave her power. So, she went on:

"What did you give him?"

"Money, of course." And Raveen nearly added, "duh" but either thought better of it or was too old to have said it in the first place.

Saffron fell silent. She had so many more questions: What money? How much? What are you talking about? But the line between building up her old relation's fraying self-esteem and trying her patience had become thin. Also, she didn't know if she could keep her own annoyance in check. So, Saffron just hung up—"ghosted," in the old-fashioned phrase—assuming Aunt Raveen wouldn't remember what had happened, anyway.

Saffron didn't ask Cornelius about it, not at first. She didn't wish to jeopardize their next encounter, which was the most intense yet, given the escalation, the consolidation of their relationship. First, she finished using a dildo, which had replaced her fingers as Cornelius' cock, her legs open, up and straddling the black arms of her swivel chair before the computer as she eased then forced then eased then forced it in and out, and he pulled himself to orgasm, Saffron swearing she could feel him pulse inside her, as she matched him coming almost to the moment.

Then both caught their breaths. Saffron lowered and crossed her legs. Cornelius' head bowed so low she felt it was a black nest like his crotch or one at the top of a tree in their jungle, so high you could only see it from the air if you were flying or falling.

"You talked to my aunt?" she asked.

"What?"

"My aunt."

Cornelius' head slowly rose. His face was so wet it was as if he had emerged from a swim in their stream. Coming, he had bit his lip so hard it bled, which he only noticed now, licking and lapping it up.

"Yes," he said.

"You asked her for something? For money?"

Cornelius nodded. Still dazed, he buttoned the shirt he had undone, then blinked a few times, reminding Saffron of a computer scrolling data as it searched for something. He looked right at her, and suddenly the glass of both screens was gone. Saffron gasped, sensing him—falsely, but did it matter?—in the same space. She smelled him but it was herself.

"I had to," he said.

"Why?"

"I was…I am in trouble."

"What kind of trouble?"

"Well—financial." Again "duh" was the next thing unspoken, in this case out of courtesy. "Temporarily."

Saffron waited, for he was the one with more to say. Cornelius waited, too, until it was obvious that he could not wait her out. Then he explained it in a rush—so quickly and jumbled that Saffron could only make out the major points, which was maybe all he wanted her to know or could bear to be known, she wasn't sure.

"I'm about to come into money…in a trust, hard to explain…Forensics is worthy work, but no one wants to pay…I'm good for it and will get it back…Very responsible person…I can get people to vouch…"

This was a different Cornelius from both the formal suitor and exciting fuck she had known. If "vulnerable" was the first word that came to mind, "desperate" was the second. Saffron fought through her disorientation— as if she were, yes, snapping aside foliage in their forest or jungle, coming into a clearing—to reach compassion, which was love, which had only been a word in old stories for her until now. He was going to be her husband, and he needed her help. Deprived of the opportunity to do so, she meant to ask but instead beseeched him: "Why didn't you come to *me*?"

Cornelius blinked one last time—not because the computer had found its reply but because it had been made to perform a separate task, easier for it was automatic.

"I was afraid," he said.

"Of what?"

"Of you."

"Why?"

"I was ashamed."

So many tears poured from his eyes it was as if a bottle of them had spilled inside him and was seeping out everywhere. Saffron had heard it was hard for two people to cry at once yet—like so many other things she had heard—it wasn't true. Seeing his humiliation, it was easy. She gulped so much she couldn't form words for a while and was still crying after he had stopped.

"You don't have to be," she said, finally.

"No?" He sounded wary.

"No. I want to do everything for you. I'll give you anything you want."

Saffron's parents had both died of the disease rioting through the world. They had left her enough money that—had she lost her job—would tide her over. This was what she now offered Cornelius. After all, she thought, her money would soon be his and vice versa.

Cornelius appeared to think seriously. His eyes no longer stared at the screen but at something higher, bigger than both of them, Saffron hoped. He shook his head with what she realized was wonder, because he didn't say no.

"Thank you," he said, his voice small, as his eyes returned to hers, then went lower, avoiding them in a different direction. He was clearly still ashamed and there was nothing she could do to change it. Once he accepted that this exchange made them equal—indistinguishable—they could take the final step, as brides and grooms had once done down actual aisles. She'd given him everything she had in all ways—he'd have to do the rest on his own. Because she loved him, she believed that he would. Saffron transferred the money to his account.

Their next date was the following night. Yet when Saffron tried to reach Cornelius online, she found that his address was unavailable. She emailed him and her letter bounced back.

For the rest of the day, Saffron sat quietly when she wasn't compulsively trying to find him. At the start, she felt there must have been a mistake. Later, as the sun set and she turned on no lights, Saffron understood that all along the error had been hers.

"Do you still not remember," she asked her aunt after one too many glasses of wine, "who gave you Cornelius' name?"

"Who's Cornelius?" Raveen asked.

"You know, the…"

"Oh, I remember—of course!"

"Who was it?"

"I meant, I remembered *him*. Not the other thing."

After she hung up, Saffron first drunkenly smashed her computer screen, then dismantled the system that had connected her to the outside world.

I came to fix it, since I was the one who'd recently done an upgrade. There were still some people who performed necessary physical tasks, covered from head to toe in what could only be called Hazmat gear.

Of course, this was just my "day job," as they used to say. My hobby—more than hobby, talent, gift, label it what you like—was programming animation, creating imaginary worlds and people online for my amusement, as well as extra income. Sometimes I'd go on a call where I could combine these two things, and those days were the best. This was what happened when I visited Raveen Bray.

The old lady was sweet but, well, addled was an unkind way to put it: she'd seen better days or seen those days more clearly, that might be most precise. She was eager to tell me all about herself and the niece who lived downstairs, about her fears for lonely Saffron's future, etc. I was, as they also used to say, all ears, even if everything on my head was as it had to be concealed.

This was how I came to create Cornelius and tell Raveen that Saffron should meet and be courted by him.

He was hardly the first man I had invented through programs and pixels. But he was my most successful achievement, the one who seemed most life-like, to have an existence independent of me, even though I controlled him as completely as had puppeteers their performers in the past. Unlike the artists who pulled those strings, though, I was nowhere to be seen and no one could know how much more physically appealing Cornelius was, maybe more appealing in all ways, than me. Yet since he was my idea, he was my essence, right?

Anyway, Saffron couldn't identify me now, either, beneath my gear, as I entered her apartment to fix what she'd destroyed. I'd been called by Aunt Raveen after she'd found my card in her keepsakes, knick-knacks and tchotchkes.

Saffron looked worse for wear than the last time I'd seen her—"through" Cornelius, of course. It seemed as if she hadn't slept at all and maybe had a few drinks too many. I sniffed for her perfume but forgot I could perceive nothing beneath my glass shield, face mask, and personal ventilator.

All of this had made her look even more attractive. As a fortune hunter, Cornelius had paid off for me enormously, but he'd been a new kind of success, too. For the first time, I'd fallen for one of the people for whom I'd conjured up a companion (mostly women but one or two men), the first time I'd ever been in love. Now I couldn't wait to tell Saffron, to do everything with her.

"Oh…right. Come in," Saffron said, backing up.

I had never minded living at a distance from people. Now I would learn why those in other centuries thought everything was better in person. I closed the door and came closer.

Penn Grows Up

Janie didn't know what to think when she saw Albertine's text. She hoped it meant that Penn was better than when they broke up, when she broke up with *him*. But maybe she was being self-aggrandizing: who was *she* to have pushed someone over the edge merely by ending a relationship? That was giving herself way too much credit. Still, Penn had gone to pieces when she told him it was over; he'd always been high-strung but this was something else, a kind of collapse—and wasn't that why she'd ended it in the first place, because it was too hard for her to cope with his way of being, his way of feeling? It had started to infect her, too, damaging her grades and her relationships with her friends and family. And since Penn was privileged enough to have been treated—genetically modified in vitro to age slower and not get diseases to which he was naturally prone—it was liable to go on *so much* longer. He would be an adolescent for *so long*, if she didn't end it now, when would she? Would she ever?

Janie was a practical, working-class person, and she had had enough drama, that was the long and short of it. And now this text from Penn's mother (from whom Janie secretly suspected Penn had inherited his instability) sent her back into the whole disaster.

If Penn was better, wouldn't he have told her so *him-self*? No, it wasn't his way to apologize—not because he was insensitive, because he was always so far into his emotions that he didn't have the distance to know what he was doing was wrong. Anyway, that's why Janie thought it plausible that Albertine was doing it *for* him.

"Could you come see him?" the text had asked.

Guiltily, Janie answered, "Yes."

When she came by the house, there was no one there—no one else, for Janie assumed that Penn was upstairs in his room. This was where behind closed doors they had first slept together—and done everything *else* before sleeping together—while his parents were out. Janie assumed that Albertine and Rudolph (which was what they always insisted she call them) knew what she and their son were doing in their home. It was another way to coddle and control him, she figured, since that's what they always did. Wasn't that why they'd paid to prolong his life in the first place?

"Penn?"

Janie called upstairs meekly, because there was a horror movie aspect to this (empty house, staircase, etc.) that freaked her out. As she ascended, she thought of all the times she had made this climb with Penn and how excited she had been, anticipating what they would do once they reached his room and closed the door. Yet today, Janie felt not even nostalgia, nothing beyond obligation, and that meant that she was really and truly over him.

"Penn?"

She stood before his door, which was half-closed, as if (she hoped) he was making progress, was halfway to entering the present and leaving the past. Maybe she could pull him all the way forward or just carefully and encouragingly follow behind him, as you would a child learning to walk. She pushed the door completely open. Either it was lighter than Janie had recalled or she'd pushed harder than she had to, for it went fast and hit the wall loudly enough to make her jump.

Penn reared up from the sheets that kind of covered him (he was only wearing shorts). In the dark room, he squinted as the light poured in, spotlighting Janie on the threshold. He'd been crying. In his sleep? With his face buried in the bed, while conscious? Janie couldn't tell. There was a weird fissure in the wall at fist-level. Had he punched it?

Janie only knew from the expression on his face (shock, dismay, disappointment, rage) that Penn was *not* better but much worse and that Albertine had wanted Janie to take him back, and that showing up was the dumbest thing Janie could have done, for there was no way that she would do it. It wouldn't have worked, anyway.

"It wouldn't have worked, anyway," she told Albertine and Rudolph later. Janie had waited downstairs for them to come home, had left poor Penn without saying a word. Maybe he'd believed he'd imagined her; she hoped so.

"You can't know that," Albertine said, agitated (as she was so often about so many things, Janie thought).

"Look," said Rudolph, ever the appeaser (Janie thought), "he'll just go away as he is, that's all."

"What do you mean, go away? Where?" Janie had no compunction about interrupting or even seeming rude, since they were no longer her boyfriend's parents or—as she had post-first orgasm imagined them—her future in-laws. She had never respected them much in the first place.

Albertine turned away, obviously to avoid answering. Since he was both more stable and more repressed (Janie thought), Rudolph replied, "Never mind."

Janie stared at the two older people. Penn had never said anything to *her* about going anywhere.

"This was your idea," she said, rage building. "You two just want to get rid of him, since he can't seem to…shape up! And you thought that I could maybe whip him into shape before he went, so you wouldn't feel too bad, that I would do your dirty work, like, like…" Later, she thought it was like cleaning a car before you sent it off a cliff. But she couldn't think of the comparison then, had been too wound-up.

"That's enough," Rudolph said, sounding a bit angry, which would have been like an explosion for anyone else and meant he was guilty. *Good*! Janie thought.

He ushered her out of the house while Albertine walked from the room, never looking back, done with Janie, accepting that she'd erred in asking her to come or expecting her to help. Janie stewed about it, stuffed in the communal car that Rudolph had somehow called (probably with a gadget he'd installed in his head; he was such a control freak, he surveilled people for a living, she thought, stewing). Still, before she was dropped off, Janie cried, hiding her face from the other passengers. She remembered Penn's tormented expression, suspected that she might never see him again or at least not for ages. He would have so much time to suffer. It wasn't his fault: he had too many years to be this age.

Janie was wrong: Albertine and Rudolph hadn't been sending Penn away to silence him or to make things easier for themselves. They were sending Penn away to make him better, because they couldn't bear his being so unhappy—Albertine couldn't, anyway. Because they knew there were risks in their plan, they'd hoped Janie might prevent them from doing it, make it unnecessary, or allow them to amend the plan and make it less extreme. But Janie had failed, this was how Albertine saw it, so they had no choice but go ahead.

Penn was not going away on a study program or what used to be called "Spring Break." He was going to have an internship on the Floater-X Space Station owned by the billionaire Seth Lupus, to whom Rudolph had sold a security system, discounted enough to secure a free room for his son. Penn was supposedly there to help researchers do space-centric drug research but really he would be given an unapproved experimental drug Lupus Labs was developing. *Tranquelle* would allow Penn to age forward and back at will in order to stop his persistent adolescence. It would be an automatic way to end or reduce the pain of his *feeling* so much.

"We have no idea what side effects the drug's going to have," a worried Albertine had told Rudolph when they first discussed it. "Because no one does."

"They've assured me won't be so bad," Rudolph said.

"Of course they're going to say that!" Albertine nearly yelled. "Because they're paying for it. And I assume we have to sign a pledge not to sue?"

Rudolph shot his wife a look which said she was right. Albertine slammed the bedroom door on him.

The Floater-X was a Transit Habitat, an inflatable research and living area connected to a Space Station. It hovered in a Lagrange Point, halfway between the Earth and the Sun or the Moon, where the gravity of the two bodies neutralized each other and allowed for a stable parking space for spacecraft. In space, crystals of proteins used in medical research could grow bigger and better and that's why they were studied up there.

Penn had always felt suspended between his parents: the force of *their* fields had created a weird stability for him, dependable and precarious at the same time. (Was his current crushingly emotional condition a way to favor his mother's side? Or was it a desperate attempt to pull away from her— even if it meant bashing himself against a wall, as it were? Or *was* it just adolescence over and over? It was unclear.) Once he was on the ship, above Albertine and Rudolph, above everyone, Penn felt more secure. If nothing else, he was too self-conscious before strangers to sob and scream as he had been doing all day on Earth. Penn was supposed to help the researchers, do their errands, and anything else they asked.

"Here," one of them said on the first day, casually handing him a specimen to bring somewhere.

Penn suspected they thought him a dilettante, the rich son of their billionaire boss's friend, which he was. In any case, he did as he was told, took the beaker of slightly warm, vaguely bubbled liquid. Was it someone's piss? Were they laughing at him? He moved down the winding corridors of the floating lab, the gravity artificial, as he feared was his own new sense of being stable.

His sleeping area had a bunk bed but elite guest that he was, no roommate. So that night, Penn alternated restlessly between the top and bottom beds, again feeling that he was halfway between mother and father or domination and submission or some other pairing outside and inside himself. He wept only late at night and then into his pillow, where his salt water was absorbed by organic and hypoallergenic cotton, the way the sea is absorbed by the sand. He had no idea how long he was meant to be there, hovering above; he hadn't thought to ask. Then he heard a soft thump at the door.

It sounded like someone had tossed something. And, in fact, when Penn rose to open up, he found a palm-sized package wrapped in white linen with a red bow curled cruelly by scissors. As he opened it, he tried not to disturb the fragile covering, but his shaking fingers shredded it and the bow crumpled to dust like an old pressed rose. Inside he found a little box which held a bottle of pills marked *Tranquelle*.

Penn assumed they were to help him sleep, but there was no one in the vicinity to ask. He faintly heard the fading motor of a scooter (the halls were wide enough to accommodate one), but maybe he had imagined it. It couldn't have been from the scientists, could it, for they had seemed to hate and resent him? Unless it was a peace offering?

There was a small round blue pill and a larger, oblong purple pill. Directions folded into nearly nothing instructed him to take one at a time. Penn took the blue.

Soon it forced him into sleep, placed unconsciousness over him like an extra blanket he didn't want. He was being suffocated—that's what it felt like, the way spies in old movies were by handkerchiefs soaked in "chloroform." Fighting, he shook his hands, which looked suddenly smaller, but he was no match for this power, whatever it was.

Penn couldn't move, was paralyzed like a newborn baby who can barely lift his head and must sleep on his stomach, so as not to choke. He found he was crying—not because he was still at the mercy of his emotions, as he had been when he'd arrived, as he'd been after breaking up with Janie, because he was doomed to adolescence—because, yes, like a baby, he'd messed himself and shit the bed. Luckily, Penn was on the bottom bunk, so his waste couldn't seep beneath him, soiling *two* mattresses. Could no one hear him crying out to be changed? Would no one come and clean him?

Penn discovered that he was not *completely* incapacitated, not yet *absolutely* the infant he feared he'd been turned into by the pill. He could still flip himself over enough times to leave the bed and land upon the floor.

There, on his stomach, he struggled as if strait-jacketed across the tiles. He aimed for the pill package which he had left upon the room's only table. Panting, propping himself up on his elbows, Penn was able to nuzzle the bottle off the surface with his nose. At last, he sent it pinging and then rolling upon a rug, where he stopped it with an extended right foot. He managed to kick the bottle close to his mouth where he fumbled with his hands—which felt tied together as if with rope—to open it. The pill popped out like a tiny, tortured turd. Penn licked it ever closer until it came between his lips and he chewed it into non-existence. It tasted like licorice, toothpaste, and dirt.

Lying there, Penn felt his stomach disturbance subside. Power began to return to his limbs. He stretched on the floor like a breaststroke swimmer. Then he found himself shuttle past normalcy into something more negative.

If the first pill had induced infancy, this one caused rapid aging. His heart pumped past adolescence to adulthood and then, terrifyingly, beyond *that*, like a subway shooting by stations with a psycho at the wheel. Eventually, at high speed, Penn's heart approached old age and the end of the line. It started to slow and slow until he could barely feel an occasional beat. At last, he waited for any beat at all.

Only a persistent banging on the door kept him conscious. As he slipped into insensibility, Penn felt a mask placed over his mouth and his body being lifted. Was he ascending even farther into space? Was he on his way to heaven? No, because he still smelled his own feces, which meant he was human and alive.

"Can you save him?" a young woman asked.

"We're going to try." This was a man.

"My father will know if you don't." It was an unpleasant promise, and so (Penn thought later) the perfect way to propel him into darkness.

Penn awoke looking into Blamey's face. Of course, he didn't know it was her, didn't know yet who this young woman was.

"What happened?" he asked.

"You lived," she said.

Only now did Penn remember the events of the night before: how he had gone from infant to old man to almost-corpse in the space of several minutes and two different kinds of pills. When he turned his head, Penn saw he was in a hospital bay, a makeshift convalescent area on the Floater-X, hooked up to fluids pumped into the veins of his hand.

The young woman hovered above him as they both did above the Earth. She had a stark, seemingly self-administered crew cut that clashed appealingly with the blemishes covering her face like constellations. They suggested she lived in a universe of her own and that's how she acted, too.

"Was I operated on?" he asked.

"Nah." She sat on the edge of his bed, not caring that she bumped him. "They just waited for it to wear off."

"For what to wear off?"

"*Tranquelle*, that stuff you took. That my father sells. Or will sell, if he ever gets it approved. You were given samples. You're not the best commercial for it, almost dying and all. I'm Blamey." She mimed shaking the hand paralyzed by tubes.

"Janie?" Not the same name as his ex-girlfriend!

"Blamey. My parents have such a hostile relationship, they named me after it. Anyway, I'm pretty sure I'm the only one on Earth named that. The only one in the universe now."

Penn noticed that she wore the same kind of wrist tag as him. Her last name was Lupus. That meant her father had employed *his* father. It also meant something else.

"What are you in the hospital for?" Penn's energy was starting to fade.

"Same as you," she shrugged. "Still being seventeen."

So, she'd been treated, too, Penn thought, given this "gift" of longevity by her parents. Blamey began receding then, shrinking in size, as if his ship was blasting off from her planet. The last thing he felt before becoming unconscious was Blamey's warm and callused palm laid upon his brow, as if checking his temperature or blessing him or both. Soon he was in the dark again, not surrounded by stars.

Penn was awakened by an elbow being jammed into his ribs. When he opened his eyes, he saw Blamey again, this time up so close she was a blur. She was not sitting but lying by his side.

"Here," she said. "Have some."

She displayed a plastic bag, the kind that held food or beverage condensed or frozen for the trip. She raised it as you would a canteen and he opened his mouth to receive what was offered. The liquid came out in beige bubbles and Penn had to chase them with his tongue like a dog to swallow. He tasted what he thought was liquor, possibly Scotch, he was no expert. Then Blamey grabbed the bag back and chug-a-lugged more confidently, the solid droplets rolling one after another as if on an invisible chute down her throat.

With her head tilted back, Penn could see long strips of scarred tissue there, like highways of unhappiness (he was already drunk and so grandiloquent). No simple suicidal wrist slashes for Blamey, he thought: with her, everything was big time.

Penn saw her scars pulse and subside, yet Blamey had stopped drinking. Small balls of tears were escaping her eyes and floating into the air or whatever was the atmosphere. They marched past Penn's face and drifted around the room (he was the only other patient). Soon there were too many to count.

"What's the matter?" he asked.

Blamey looked at him, her eyes expelling more clear bobbing balls. She couldn't say and only mouthed the answer: "Seventeen."

Penn understood and his tears joined hers. All of them hung in the air like a bouquet of bad feelings before popping one by one. Penn realized that the artificial gravity had been eliminated or repealed or whatever you did with artificial gravity. Or was it just the liquor that made him see things this way?

Like him, Blamey was the embodiment of what used to be called adolescent angst. Both he and she would be trapped in this condition for who knew how long?—it would seem like forever—and they had recognized each other after barely being introduced. Both were now suspended above everything, sensing and suffering.

Yet unlike other people—Janie, Albertine and Rudolph, even Penn himself before he came aboard—Blamey celebrated this state. She apparently believed that her excess of anxiety, anguish, and excitement was a form of euphoria, something that placed her *above* other people, even if she was in agony. That's how it felt when she reached over and kissed him, pressed her tongue into his mouth as if to deposit herself in him. Soon he did the same to her, Blamey holding and stroking his face as he penetrated her mouth and drew back. They became each other's time capsule.

Suddenly, they were bubbles, too, floating in the air, levitated by emotions so many and so uncontrollable they gave Penn and Blamey buoyancy. Their clothes were floating, too, as they removed them, sailing above the hospital beds like birds—no, as if they were underwater, Blamey's large breasts, Penn's long, swollen penis suspended, moving in slow motion as their parts brushed against and by each other. Blamey pulled his erection as if it was a lever that opened her and everything else, directing him inside her, completing their sense of being the same. Then their tears were joined by the white balls of his semen as they disengaged, both spinning like the zits on her face, the stars in the sky, the air or whatever was this atmosphere filled with extended adolescence.

Blamey let Penn sleep it off. Then she badgered him awake again. It was night by now and everyone else was asleep—though it didn't matter, the boss' daughter could do as she pleased. They flew nude from the hospital to a lab where Blamey kept the lights off and mounted Penn on a swivel chair, after tying his hands down with gravity straps. Gripping the chair's arms as she fucked him, Penn screamed something incoherent when he came, too excited for words. Afterwards, she wound herself around him, hugging him to stay grounded. Penn's hair, which was long, slithered as if at the bottom of the sea but Blamey's hair was too short to move at all.

"I'm so happy we met," she said.

"Me, too."

"You're the only one who wants this like I do. My father tried to give me *Tranquelle*, that willful aging junk your parents gave you. But I said, get lost."

Penn heard this with unease. He hadn't known that Albertine and Rudolph were behind his drugging. He wasn't sure how he felt about it, so he stayed silent. Also, he wasn't sure if he wanted what Blamey wanted. Yet he wanted Blamey. So, he continued not to speak.

"There's a different drug onboard that's also not approved," she said. "*Minora*. This one works. And the approval is just a matter of time."

"Yes?"

Blamey nodded. She scrambled for the drawer of the desk by their side, pressing in a security code. Penn realized she had not chosen this lab by accident. Had she even come onboard for this very reason, to get this pill?

"Here," she said, and now there were two pink tablets in her palm.

"What does it do?"

"It will officially keep us this age forever."

Blamey hadn't hesitated with the answer, hadn't hedged or pretended otherwise. Before he could respond, she'd passed him a pill.

"Can you take it without water?" she asked. "Or should we go get some from the kitchen?"

Now that his sexual fever had subsided and morning was on its way, Penn felt weird flying around the ship naked. Yet that wasn't the reason he paused.

"I can do it without water," he said, answering just the practical part of her question. And now that he'd said he *could* take it, Blamey assumed that he would. She had been waiting to share this way of life, this intensity for eternity or at least until the day way in the future when she died. Did Penn want it for that long, too, want it never to end?

As he was considering it, Blamey placed a *Minora* on her tongue. It stuck on the end, which she wiggled at him. Then she pulled it in, shut her mouth and swallowed. She made an "it's nasty" face before she shrugged the taste away, accepting it as a rite of passage she was tough enough to endure.

"Okay, big boy," she said. "Your turn."

Penn couldn't act, stunned by his own fear. He was reminded of that play he had been assigned in school about teenage lovers where the girl thought the boy was dead and killed herself but the boy was still alive, or something. The expression on his face—which he realized later was begging her forgiveness—told Blamey all she needed to know.

Blamey's own expression wasn't angry or sad. She simply pulled the pill from Penn's fingers and squeezed his hand once before turning. He realized: she would do this without him; with him it would have just been less lonely. Leaving balls of tears behind, Blamey flew away, as the naked, crying, and coming teenager she wished always to remain.

Penn sat there for a while, also naked yet still tied down. He was surprised that he wasn't made broken-hearted by this, as he was by everything that didn't make him aroused. He sensed that this new equanimity signaled the start of a new phase, the advent at last of growing older. He managed to free himself.

That day, Blamey had the ship turn around and make the months-long trip back to Earth. She had given the captain a new order, or at least Penn assumed she had, for nothing else made sense. They dropped him off alone when they arrived.

As he disembarked, Penn caught a glimpse of her mingling with the others. Blamey glanced at him once, with fondness and regret. It was as if she were helping someone older cross a street, performing an act of mercy for an elder.

Six months later, Albertine died. She suffered a heart attack, which had not been averted by the pills she took to prevent such an event. It was as if her anxiety was so great there was only so much a medicine could do. Or maybe everything—no matter how prolonged or forestalled by surgery and drugs—always came to an end, anyway.

Not long after, Penn was invited to lunch at a local diner. Having heard about Albertine, Blamey had come looking for him, using directions from her father.

Penn noticed that the restaurant's lights had bleached out and made her blemishes imperceptible. Or was she wearing makeup? Or had they disappeared on their own? Blamey's hair was growing out, too. Penn secretly felt she'd been more striking with the buzzcut that made her resemble that movie character who got burned at the stake, he couldn't remember her name.

Of course, being burned alive by their ages had been what linked them aboard the Floater-X. Now Penn had begun to cool, as it were. To his surprise, so had Blamey.

To begin with, she'd changed her name. "Why, she wondered, "should I represent my parents' recriminations?" She'd become B., because the letter was almost but not quite at the beginning of things, just like her.

"Not bad," Penn said and kept his doubts to himself. Knowing Blamey—B.—involved not saying everything he thought.

Her behavior, too, had begun to calm. She was no longer flailing and flying around, not just because she was back on the Earth.

"What happened to that other drug?" Penn asked. "*Minora?* I thought you were going to be…" He meant to say, seventeen forever, but she cut him off.

"Snake oil," B. said, using an archaic expression that had survived. "But that won't keep my dad from marketing it."

Penn nodded, surprised—not that the drug hadn't worked—that she accepted its failure and what it meant for her future. Their timing for moving on had turned out to be the same. Yet what would they make of each other when they weren't both on fire?

"Look," B. said, "I'd like to keep knowing you."

"Me, too," Penn said, quickly. Before this moment, he hadn't been able to admit his loneliness, even to himself. Was it losing his mother, whom he so resembled? He wasn't sure. Impatient tears fell from his eyes like dogs released from cages in a race. B. reached out and held his hand—hers was still callused and still warm—until he stopped. Penn blinked out what he felt would be his last tears for a while, then dried his cheeks with the back of his hands.

"Good," she said. "Now let's wolf this down. I really want to sleep with you again. Let's get started."

Penn nodded. Feeling human, alive, and no longer so very young, he signaled the robot server for their check.

Acknowledgments

Short stories are hard to write, harder to publish, and impossible to collect. I'm truly grateful to Cornerstone Press for creating the Legacy Series, making books of stories available to all those (like me) who love the form. I'd like to acknowledge publisher Dr. Ross Tangedal, senior editor Paige Biever, and Sophie McPherson and Sam Bjork in sales/media for doing an excellent job in every aspect of this gutsy endeavor. I'd also like to salute the students at University of Wisconsin-Stevens Point for their careful and insightful work in reading and editing. My total ignorance about how to correctly use commas has convinced me never to use them again.

These stories were first published in small magazines, both online and in print, some of which are already defunct. At this writing, America is abandoning its investment in the not-for-profit arts, so many more of these publications will soon be gone. Maybe many more will also be created, since they're fueled not by greed, ambition, or ideology but by love, which no government, no matter how awful, can legislate. I gratefully acknowledge the following publications:

"Obsolescence" was published in *Adelaide*
"Endless" was published in *Gone Lawn*
"Spirit" was published in *Sequestrum*

"Appropriate" was published in *Pioneertown*
"Chip" was published in *Expanded Field*
"Simultaneously" was published in *Epoque Press E-zine*
"Gift" was published in *Oyez Review*
"Empathy" was published in *Lowestoft Chronicle*
'Repair" was published in *Identity Theory*
"Entertaining" was published in *Pigeon Review*
"Einzelheit" was published in *Sortes*
"Reality" was published in *Permafrost*
"Redemption" was published in *The Opiate*
"Nucleus" was published in *Switchback* and *Tamarind*
"The Freelancer" was published in *Gargouille* and *Penumbric*
"The New Year's Resolution" was published in *Vol. I Brooklyn*
"The Image of His Parents" was published in *Idle Ink*
"Doubles Alley" was published in *Teleport* and *Aethlon*
"In Person" was published in *Two Thirds North*
"Penn Grows Up" was published in *Anomaly*

Speaking of love, I'd finally like to thank my wife, Susan Kim, for supporting me…in all ways. I know I already dedicated the book to her, but that only proves I can never thank her enough.

Laurence Klavan is the Edgar Award-winning writer of *Mrs. White* (writing as Margaret Tracy w/ Andrew Klavan), *The Cutting Room*, and *The Family Unit and Other Fantasies*. His musical, *Bed and Sofa*, written with Polly Pen, received two Obie Awards and nominations from the Drama Desk, Outer Critics Circle, and the New York Drama Critics. His short fiction has been widely published in *Alaska Quarterly Review, The Literary Review, Conjunctions, Vol. I Brooklyn, Beloit Fiction Journal, Louisville Review,* and elsewhere. His work for young people (written with his wife, Susan Kim) includes the graphic novels, *City of Spies* and *Brain Camp*, and the YA fiction trilogy, *Wasteland, Wanderers,* and *Guardians*. He and Kim live in New York City.